HELL BENT

THE GUILD OF SHADOWS 2

MARIE BILODEAU

This book is a work of fiction. Any resemblance to persons, living or dead, or places, events or locations is purely coincidental.

Cover art by Éric Belisle.

Cover design by Ânia Loureiro.

Editing by Jessica Torrance.

To Derek Künsken,
whose friendship programming is infectious.

ACKNOWLEDGMENTS

I'm always humbled by all the support I receive. It takes a village to raise a book! Since I wrote a few books in this series in one quick succession, I'm forced (forced!) to repeat a lot of my thanks.

First off, Tira became fleshed out thanks to the people surrounding the Dungeons and Dragon table, and how they interacted with her. She became who she is thanks to my #writersintaldorei crew – Brandon Crilly, Jay Odjick, Evan May, Derek Künsken, Tyler Goodier, Nicole Lavigne and Matt Moore.

A bunch of the characters in this novel are based on the characters skillfully played by them, though the story, world and everything else is very much not at all it.

We ended arc 1 of our campaign after almost two years. I wasn't ready to let go of these characters, both the ones who lived, and the ones who perished along the journey. (You can read all about that at www.mariebilodeau.com/dd-taldorei/, should you be interested.)

This is my chance to play with them again, and give Tira an entirely new direction to grow into.

Aside from my game buddies, I also couldn't have finished this book without Kerri Elizabeth Gerow, who has supported me for the length of my career and still seems to love me. Same for my sister-in-law, Jessica Torrance, who was instrumental in forging this book, both as its editor and head cheerleader.

And of course, my maman Suzanne Desjardins, for her eternal support. My writing BFF Linda Poitevin, for continuously inspiring me to level up. And my brother, Jean-François Bilodeau, because he's just so damn fun.

And to you, dearest reader, for coming along this insane journey with me.

THE DAGGER FLEW at a lazy angle, not even trying to hit its target. I sidestepped equally as lazily, not bothering to take cover, and threw a dagger back toward the assailant.

It went wide. Embarrassingly wide, even.

We'd been training for more than three hours. I might not have been at my best, and this whole thing lacked a certain sense of urgency.

Turned out that I sucked at training.

Someone gasped beside me and I turned to see Rachel go down, her pale skin almost luminous even in the darkness. Poor Rachel. She couldn't see in the dark and had just taken a hit in the gut.

Her assailant came in for a second blow, but I stepped in, grabbed his arm and pulled him back.

Don't hit a girl while she's down, jackass.

I yanked him back, wrenching his shoulder. He grunted, but didn't go down, kicking my legs out from under me.

Ouch.

That was exactly what had happened last time, which proved doubly frustrating. This time, instead of kicking back, I pushed myself sideways to roll out of hitting range, pulled a dagger, and sent it flying in the general direction of the attacker.

A satisfying thunk and grunt.

I pushed myself up and looked in the direction my knife had flown. The attacker was still standing and came my way.

Oh shit. I hadn't hit the right target.

Orienting after tumbling was damn hard! I leapt sideways, moved to meet my attacker, and tripped him. He managed to fall into a roll and took cover beside a half wall.

"You hit me!" Rachel said, sounding pretty pissed. I winced. Well, now I knew what I'd hit. Still, a pissed Rachel wasn't great for anyone involved.

"Sorry," I offered, trying to both apologize to Rachel while avoiding the arrow flying my way. The trainers' shots were getting a bit *less* lazy, which proved worrisome. "I didn't mean to," I said in half a whisper. My breath burned my throat, and every limb ached.

The other initiates were gone, already knocked out

(sometimes quite literally). Rachel and I were still here but flagging like hell, and we knew it.

"Tira," she choked the word out.

I knew that sound. Rachel was hurt, and tired, and probably pissed as hell.

That was *definitely* not good.

"Gangway!" I screamed, and threw myself behind a half wall, which had been a full wall a few sessions ago. It had *almost* withstood Rachel then.

The darkness suddenly lit up with shades of pink, sparkles fluttering in the air. It would have been pretty, if I didn't know what was coming next.

The training alarm rang, the lights were thrown on, and someone screamed to take cover.

I ignored it all and crouched with my arms hugging my head, the sparkles shooting lightning bolts one into the other, until the entire area erupted with blinding light. The half wall shattered beside me, sending me sprawling to the ground, debris crumbling atop me.

Stay down stay down stay down I repeated over and over like a mantra. The effect lasted at least an agonizing ten seconds. Getting up probably meant death.

The light grew brighter. *Fuck.*

I blocked my ears and opened my mouth. I'd seen one guy's lung explode the first time this had gone off. After that, we'd received special training just to survive our own teammate.

3

I closed my eyelids as tightly as I could, exploding light searing my eyes anyway. The entire room exhaled as the air was sucked out. My lungs hurt, but I waited, knowing this would only take a second.

The air blasted back in, claiming the vacuum created by the explosion. That's what got you, if you weren't paying attention. The second, bigger explosion.

I rolled at least ten feet and came to a stop on my back.

Someone coughed to the side.

"Clear!" Someone managed to croak out.

I opened my eyes and sat up, pushing pieces of drywall and metal off me. A few Guild operatives, aka our trainers, did the same, their dark clothes covered in dust. A few scrapes adorned me, but aside from that, I seemed unarmed.

Not bad!

I grinned and took stock to see how everyone else had fared.

Rachel knelt in the middle of her devastation, a dagger sticking out of her shoulder (oops). She looked as ruined as the room around her.

"Let's call it a day," Dame Zallir said with her cracking voice, a blend of jazz lounge singer and military commander. She stepped into the training room, looking pretty much like both, green-streaked raven hair tumbling in messy waves down to her waist, dark skin covered by military fatigues. She didn't wear the Guild of Shadows' customary black outfit, nor could I spot the tell-tale infinity symbol anywhere on her.

As far as I could tell, she was perfectly human. A perfectly scary, well-trained human.

I walked over to Rachel and knelt beside her. She winced as she pulled out the dagger, blueish blood oozing lazily where the wound already began to heal.

"Sorry about hitting you," I said. I wished that I'd grabbed a first aid kit so I could at least dampen the flow of blood. Thankfully, it was doing just fine at slowing down without any gauze.

I envied her that particular ability, though the rest of her powers made looking like a demon seem relaxing.

"No worries," she shrugged. "You pissed me off, though," she looked embarrassed at her own outburst.

"Understandably." I helped her up. She handed me the dagger, and I flipped it into my belt. Unlike at Margrave Academy, where I'd spent my first few years as a Traded on this planet, we could keep our weapons here.

At the Guild of Shadows. The place where I'd been shuffled off to, after a long and exhausting—not to mention damn weird and convoluted – trial. I had so many questions, but no answers were forthcoming. For three months, we'd been training. I hadn't seen the outside of these walls except one time, and it had been made clear that I would be watched more closely.

I sighed as Rachel and I limped out. We were exhausted and still had no idea what we were doing here. Except for training. And staying alive. After a few failed exercises, it had been made amply clear that our survival was not assured.

I passed by Dame Zallir, admiring the depth of her eyes, the assuredness in her relaxed stance, the way she seemed to know exactly who she was.

And *what* she was.

Human. She belonged here, unlike us Traded: random species from worlds far away, probably not marked on any star charts. A twist of fate following a weird portal incident that no one understood or could replicate.

All I knew was that I looked like a demon, with purple skin, small horns, dark hair. It was a hell of a thing to look like when trapped on this world.

"I'm going to get checked out by the medic," Rachel said, and bid me goodbye. I turned to her, her pale blueish skin framed by short pink hair the only outward sign that she herself was a Traded. She looked perfectly human otherwise, unlike me. Well, the blue blood gave her away, too.

"I'll see you later," I waved her off, heading down a secondary corridor toward our rooms. The Guild let us have our own rooms, to allow us space to reflect.

Not that I took advantage of that, but I certainly enjoyed having my own space.

"Tira," Ian said, falling in step beside me. He was dressed in his dark Guild outfit, his long brown hair tied back and his beard slightly unkempt. Ian didn't love hair, probably because he could shapeshift into animals and did so as often as he could.

He didn't have to do anything with his hair as an animal.

"Ian," I grinned at him. I hadn't seen him in almost a month and had been worried about him. Ian was second-in-command of the Guild, a role he didn't relish and one that Sonsil, the leader of the Guild, seemed to impose on him for reasons that weren't completely clear to anyone.

But Ian *was* the reason I was here. He'd been assigned to make sure I joined the Guild. Or made it here, since it wasn't much of a choice. To make sure my past friendship with my best friend Clay didn't get in my way.

I had issues with Ian. But nobody was perfect, and he was as trapped as I was.

"I'd like you in a briefing," Ian said, his voice low. My eyebrows raised and I glanced his way, my heart beating faster as my grin widened. Was I about to actually get out of here for a bit? Briefings led to missions, right?

My body practically vibrated with enthusiasm, a

fact that didn't escape Ian, who shook his head and sighed.

"Don't get your hopes up, Tira," he growled. That only made me grin more. Grumpy Ian meant it would probably be dangerous.

"What is it?" I asked, ignoring his comment. I'd *barely* disobeyed orders since getting here.

"Meet me in the Mission Room in fifteen minutes," he said, looking me up and down. "Maybe come with a bit less wall dust on you."

I looked down, my black uniform covered in dust.

I shrugged. "I look terrible in white anyway."

Ian nodded distractedly, mumbled that he'd see me soon, and headed down another corridor. I kept course, heading to my room to clean up and change quickly.

I couldn't help but smile as I got dressed. I was more than ready for some fun and, from Ian's dark mood, this would undoubtedly be fun.

2

I'D NEVER ACTUALLY BEEN in the Mission Room until now, and whatever I'd expected, it wasn't this.

It looked like a classroom. Several of us were invited to sit in rows of about thirty tables and chairs. Only half the seats were taken, and precious few of those with faces I knew.

It would be nice if the Guild believed in some sort of team-building exercise. We were expected to run into battle and have each other's backs, to follow orders and work seamlessly together, and yet they didn't seem to think it important for us to know one another.

It's not like there would ever be more of us. We were it. One bunch of babies traded twenty years ago. Cribs that had held human babies just moments before suddenly filled with monsters, from worlds they hadn't even known existed.

One time. One giant multi-planetary burp. The humans assumed, maybe out of parental despair, that their kids were on our planets (wherever the hell those were), and that those parents had taken care of their kids, just as they had us.

Or so they like to say. Most of us were locked away in "schools," taught to fight, to obey, to prepare to be shunted into guilds, organizations and leagues, to be kept in check for the rest of our days. While being useful to humanity.

It was the price we paid for our survival here. They'd never made clear what would happen if we sidestepped, but I'd seen enough at the school alone to know that the price would be high.

I never imagined it might be this boring, though.

I looked from my desk to Ian, shifting in my seat to get more comfortable. Having a devil tail made sitting comfortably tough at times, especially in shitty old chairs.

Ian had helped me find my way to the Guild. He'd saved my life a few times, and I'd saved his. But he'd been operating under the Guild of Shadows without my knowing, apparently not having gone to school, but recruited more quickly.

He'd been vital in my split from Clay.

Clay.

I missed Clay. I didn't blame Ian for our split. Clay had wanted different things than I did, and he was happy in his fighter's league. And Clay had kept a *lot* of secrets from me. Once those secrets had started to unravel, well, it was hard to hold it all together.

In the end, I knew that I could only trust Clay so far. Just like I could probably trust Ian so far. Both were thick with secrets and lies, which scratched the shiny veneer of friendship. Of course, both could only trust me so far, too.

I sighed, glanced around at the boring décor.

I needed more friends. Maybe Rachel would be my new friend. She was explosively fun. I spotted her two rows ahead on the other side of the room, and she gave me a suspicious smile.

Could work out.

"Good morning," Sonsil said as he stepped in. Tall, dark-skinned, bald head, and piercing eyes, I still wasn't sure if he was Traded or human.

Sonsil stood in front of the class, pausing to look each of us in the eye, as though gauging us. Everyone stood straighter, except me. I leaned back in my seat. Sitting straight in a chair was great, but not the most useful ability. Sonsil paused on me a tad longer, and I swore a slight smile tugged at his lips.

Before I could analyze it further, it had vanished, and he was all business again.

He glanced to Ian and nodded, stepping aside to

cede the front to him. Now I slid forward in my seat. I'd never really seen how Ian and Sonsil operated together, and I found it fascinating. Ian was supposedly second-in-command of the Guild, but he seemed to be more concerned with recruits and individual members than the overall Guild. It struck me as strange, but what did I know about operations? I'd been trapped in battle training all this time.

I'd have to learn by watching, since no one bothered telling us anything.

"The Rosetta Guild was attacked yesterday," Ian said without preamble, his voice low but direct, clearly reaching the back of the class. A few initiates gasped. I had no clue what the Rosetta Guild was or did, but I didn't like the idea of a guild being attacked.

Ian continued before we could ask questions, holding up his palm to stop any that might have blurted out.

"We don't have many details, except that it was fast, and cruel." He paused, seemed to ponder his next move, then nodded to a Guild operative standing near the computer at the front.

I could see the warning form on Ian's lips, as though he wanted to tell us to brace ourselves. Instead, he just stepped out of the viewing field of the screen as it lit up, first blue as it connected to the computer.

Ian stepped to the other side than Sonsil. The leader gave him a slight nod, as though backing his play.

The screen changed from blue and gasps erupted from around the room as images filled the screen.

A body sliced in two, blood red as a human's puddled between the two halves, orange eyes staring up without seeing, green skin sickly yellowed.

The next picture popped up before we could analyze it too much. I glanced at Rachel. She was pale. Well, paler than usual, her lips thin in concentration as she tried to grasp useful details.

I turned back to the pictures. The Rosetta Guild had a lot of books and computers and the bodies, sliced through in one form or another, were all presumably Traded.

All of them wore simple linen robes, which I guess were that guild's look. I was glad for black, personally. The bodies offered few clues, except that the assailants had been quick. A few victims had obviously tried to run, cut down from behind. But quite a few had been in groups, as though they'd been chatting or working on various books and documents.

The background revealed a lot more. Opened doors that were unbreached, like running hadn't been an option. Books still on bookshelves, even mugs left on desks, furniture unflipped. No bodies beneath tables, desperately trying to hide only to be murdered there.

It had been *damn* quick.

The pictures stopped on two Traded cut apparently

at the same time, toppled together in a jumble of limbs, green blood mixing with red.

Shit, this was pretty gross stuff. I tore my eyes away and tried to focus on the students, as Ian asked if anyone had any questions.

What the hell was that?" was the only immediate question on my mind, so I held my peace and gathered my thoughts.

"What's the Rosetta Guild?" an initiate asked. Grag, I think was his name. He looked unremarkably human, which was a blessing for most Traded.

Ian nodded. "They're an information and research guild, feeding the rest of us important information on political divides, worrisome developments in media, dangerous situations that need to be dealt with. The kind of stuff that makes sure we target the right things and people."

"Is there more than one guild like that?" A full-fledge operative asked. I had no clue who they were, though I loved their makeup: purple around the entire eye, matching purple lips. It might not be makeup. Hard to tell with the Traded.

"There are," Ian said, though he provided no further information. Even operatives weren't privy to all the info, it seemed.

We waited in silence, neither Ian nor Sonsil offering to break it, both apparently comfortable with limitless quantities of it.

"How long ago did this happen?" someone broke the silence finally.

"About two hours ago," Ian answered. I sat straighter and leaned forward. The move didn't escape Ian.

"Question, Ms. Misu?" he raised an eyebrow.

"More of an observation," I shrugged. He didn't stop me, so I went ahead. I hated the attention I'd inadvertently drawn to myself. All those eyes on me...I fought the urge to fold the shadows around me and vanish.

"They were all killed quickly," I said as a matter of fact, though that seemed to take a lot of the other students by surprise. I didn't feel the need to elaborate. "So we can assume it was more than one assailant, although all bearing the same sharp blades." I paused, another possibility springing to life. "Or, one *really* fast assailant."

Ian didn't stop me, waiting for me to continue. Everyone's eyes were on me, and I could feel my purple deepen with embarrassment. I pushed through.

"So, if this happened just two hours ago, and I assume there's no trail to follow," Ian gave a slight nod. I figured we'd be hunting them down otherwise, "that means they're fast, silent, and deadly," I paused, looked at Ian. "Who would do that so effectively?"

He held my gaze. I waited, not looking away. Two could play at the staring game.

"Who do you think?" he asked softly, though his voice held the edge that confirmed my suspicions.

"I don't think humans could pull this off," I said simply, avoiding responding more directly.

Traded.

Traded had hunted down other Traded and massacred them. The room grew hushed with the realization that humans were not the only ones we had to fear.

"We don't think humans did this either," Ian said. "Which is why we need to be extra careful. The Rosetta Guild wasn't without its defenses."

"Why would Traded hunt down other Traded?" Rachel asked, and I glanced at Sonsil and Ian. They gave absolutely no outward sign of flinching, even though I knew the Guild of Shadows would do it as needed. To maintain the balance between Traded and humans.

An assassins' league, but we wouldn't call it that. Too negative, I guess. Poor marketing material.

"We intend to find out," Ian said. I noticed that Sonsil was looking at me. I guess I was one of the few here who'd gotten a full debrief on the Guild of Shadows. I held his gaze, hoping I made it clear that I had no intention of sharing that knowledge with anyone else here. I hadn't yet. I didn't feel any motivation to do so now.

And it was pretty clear that not everyone had been

privy to the same recruitment pitch. I could ponder for hours what that meant about the Guild of Shadows, but it was pretty clear to me that it said a lot more about me and my inclinations.

It wasn't worth worrying about those. I hadn't yet. Wasn't time to start.

I nodded to Sonsil, and he returned the slight gesture.

"No outings," Ian glanced my way. Sheesh, sneak out once, and everyone thought you were the worst culprit. It's not like I'd been the only one to ever sneak out, right? Surely not!

"No risks. Stay inside, be alert. If we do fall under attack, let the senior operatives support you. Hide. Don't play heroes so early on in your training."

A few boastful mumbles around me made it clear that many here believed they were ready to take on any assailant. But we were all trainees, so it didn't matter how good we thought we were.

Unless the higher-ups believed us ready, we were effectively benched.

"Have other guilds been warned?" I asked, and Ian's eyes softened. He knew my best friend, Clay, was a member of the Wolf Pack League, not too far from here. The only time I'd snuck out was to cheer Clay on in one of his arena battles.

"They have," Ian said, his voice quieter than I

anticipated it would be. "We're all going to help each other stay safe."

And just like that, we had been told that we were targets to some really successful murderers.

And then, we were dismissed.

3

Rachel fell in beside me as I walked out of the room. She didn't say anything but seemed as eager as me to get away from the boasting students.

Sure you could take them on, buddy.

I'd seen these people in battle. Not all training had been equal. Rachel was pretty good, though, if at times a little out of control. It just made her more interesting, to my mind.

I glanced her way but didn't speak. The silence suited us both. Our rooms were near each other, and she wasn't bad company.

I didn't really want to chat, anyway. My mind kept reeling back to those pictures: the precision of the cuts, the still-full coffee mug on the desk, the books spattered with blood, pages unread and still wet...it had been fast, almost merciful. No one had suffered.

Barely anyone had had the chance to notice what was happening. The few that did only had the chance to turn around and run a few steps.

I wondered if they'd been caught so unaware because they weren't a fighter's league. Because they'd been trained differently. What had their defenses been like? Ian said they'd been defended but hadn't exactly elaborated.

I imagined the Guild of Shadows was well defended. From the little I'd seen breaking in (unsuccessfully) back when I didn't realize this was even the Guild of Shadows, getting in here would be difficult. I hoped impossible, but I doubted that.

What kind of defenses did Clay's league have?

"Sorry about the explosion," Rachel interrupted my thoughts. I stared at her in confusion. I'd forgotten she was even there.

"Oh, no worries," I shrugged. "I mean, I did throw a dagger at you."

"Ya," she said. Her shoulder seemed fine now. On top of her freaky good ability to heal, they had several Traded here who could heal others, which proved useful when our training involved real weapons.

Most of us were trained already, thanks to our "schooling." The Margrave Academy had been my own little hell for several years. Clay had been the only good thing to come out of there.

I missed him. I hadn't seen him in over a month. I

hoped he was safe. I hoped he wasn't doing anything stupid, like signing up for death battles. The glory was bigger, sure, but I wasn't a fan of the death part.

I knew they streamed the combats, but we weren't given access to any outside media. Not back when we were in school, and not now. I'd seen people go around with their smartphones and glasses, watches and rings, but I'd never been privy to one. Most were calibrated to biometrics, so it's not like stealing one would make it work for me.

Plus, a lot of them didn't even work for Traded. Touchscreens didn't respond, or they were awkward to hold with claws. This world wasn't built for us, and they'd focused their energies on making us adapt, instead of adapting it to us.

"I wonder why they went after the Rosetta Guild?" Rachel asked. I frowned.

"I assume because they were Traded?"

She shrugged. "Maybe. But my captain always said that assuming was dangerous business. The seas can change pretty quickly."

"Your captain?" I didn't know a lot of people's stories, but I'd certainly never heard one involving a captain. "Like, your lover?"

She laughed a clear laugh. "No, like my ship captain."

"You come from a ship?" I stopped in front of my room.

"I do," she said softly. "I was abandoned at a pier, left to die on the water. A trading vessel found me—one of those giant behemoths—and the captain took me in. Raised me," she paused, as though gathering her thoughts. "I miss the sea. I hate being stuck here. I hate not being on the ship with my crew."

"I get that," I said. "I miss my best friend. Couldn't you have stayed on your ship?"

"No. All Traded had to join a guild or league," her inflection indicated that she hadn't been given much of a choice as to which one she'd join, either. "Even those of us who had loving families." She blushed, and added, "the few of us."

"That sucks," I offered. I didn't really know what else to say. I mean, the Guild so far hadn't been any worse than the Academy. In lots of ways, it was better. Except for missing Clay, of course.

Everything else was pretty much a giant life upgrade. Not sleeping in a cell was fantastic. I had more clothes. All black, sure, but I looked good in black. And no one beat me up. Like, outside of training.

Plus, the control tattoo on the side of my neck, used to incite pain by the Margrave Academy, hadn't been used once at the Guild, even though I was fairly certain that they had the control mechanism to use it.

Why wouldn't they have it, after all? Once a Traded, always a Traded.

"Tira!" Ian's voice stopped us short. Rachel hesitated

but stayed, maybe out of curiosity. Couldn't blame her for that.

Ian joined us, nodding to Rachel. He didn't dismiss her, which I'd half expected. He didn't even seem to mind that she stayed. Rachel's blue-tinged skin glowed a little brighter. Her eyes certainly did. Like she didn't intend to miss a word of this conversation.

"I want to make sure you're clear that you're not to leave unless ordered to do so," Ian said, his voice soft yet granular.

"I heard," I said, though I couldn't hide the disappointment in my voice.

"You can contact Clay," Ian said, looking amused. I grinned. We were rarely allowed to use outside communications, though full operatives seemed to be given smartphones.

I was looking forward to that stage.

"And then," he added, "come back to your room, and stay there. Don't leave until you're told to." He looked over to Rachel, targeting her with the same dark look. "The same goes for all initiates."

"Understood," Rachel said, and I thought she might salute for a second.

"Don't do anything stupid," Ian practically growled. Which made sense, since he could change into a dog or other animals at will. Well, mostly at will. He didn't seem able to fully control it, sometimes getting trapped in animal shape, or not able to turn back.

Still, better than Rachel's lack of control.

"I won't," I said, and meant it. Mostly because I knew I couldn't get away with it. Like, if there was even a ten per cent chance of success, I might try it. But there wasn't, and Ian had probably come here to let me know that.

"Thanks for letting me call Clay," I said, making it clear that I understood a bribe when I heard one.

He nodded to me, then to Rachel, before turning around without another word and heading down the corridor.

"He's interesting," Rachel said once he was gone.

"He's nice," I replied. Ian had helped make sure I survived long enough to make it to the Guild. He'd helped me break free from Clay, when we both would have gotten killed if we'd hung on to each other.

My heart skipped a beat. That parting still hurt.

Before we'd both left to join our guilds, we'd shared a quick kiss, Clay and me. I flushed just thinking about it, my purple growing deeper.

If Rachel noticed, she was kind enough not to mention it. I made note of that. Kindness seemed to be in short supply for most people.

"He's the second-in-command of the Guild of Shadows," Rachel said softly. "How nice can he be?"

I cocked my head a bit and looked at her. "As nice as he can be, under the circumstances?"

"Fair enough," Rachel said. She seemed to want to

say something else, but held back. "Well, I guess I'd best head into my room."

"I'll go call Clay," I said.

We parted and I headed to the communal social room. The room, even though currently empty, always smelled like hot dogs. Multiple couches lined the walls, and shelves held books, a TV and some movies and games. Enough to keep us entertained and yet disconnected.

A single phone sat on the small desk, the line undoubtedly monitored. It was old-school rotary, to boot. A pen lay beside it, for the initiates and operatives whose non-human fingers couldn't fit into the smaller holes to turn it. Good luck if the headset didn't fit your head, though.

I dialed. The phone rang twice, and Jolene picked up. I both liked and hated her. She was really nice, which was annoying. But I couldn't tell if she saw Clay as a friend or a potential lover. That part annoyed me a lot more than I cared to admit.

"Hey Jolene," I said cheerfully. She was Clay's friend, after all, and she'd always been nice to me, too. Infuriatingly so.

"Oh, hey Tira," she said, her usually cheerful tones muted.

"You heard?" I asked.

"Ya. Scary stuff."

"You guys put up more security?" The last time I'd

broken into their league, well, breaking in wasn't necessary. They were a fighter's league, I'd been informed. Why would they need security? They could just beat people up! That thought still made me want to roll my eyes.

"We did," she gave a low chuckle. "Though I think the Boss is repulsed at the idea."

I didn't like the Boss one bit. She didn't care about the Traded the way Sonsil did, or at least the way I thought he did. She was cold-blooded, and had almost killed Clay and I.

Her, I'd like to hurt.

"Good," I said, relieved to hear that. "Is Clay around?"

"He is," she bid me farewell and put me on hold.

I shifted in my chair, trying to get more comfortable. The room was empty, but I knew an operative probably wasn't far. Or they might be watching me on some kind of security camera. They were certainly listening on the line.

I couldn't trust that anything I said here would remain private.

"Tira," Clay said, sounding out of breath.

"You okay?" I asked, sitting partly out of my chair, as though I could leap to protect him from whatever threatened him.

"Oh ya," he said. I could hear the grin in his voice.

"Was just practicing. You should see some of the new moves I'm learning!"

"I wish I could," I said. I missed him so bad and hearing his voice without being able to see him made it even worse. I imagined him, could picture every detail of his face. His unkempt hair, his dark eyes, his slightly sharpened teeth and claw-like hands. Clay had been my best friend since we'd met. Hell, he'd been my only friend for a long time.

I wasn't about to forget him.

"Did you hear about the Rosetta Guild?"

"I did," he said, his voice immediately more serious. "You keeping safe?"

I shrugged, then sighed. Phone conversations were so stifling and dependent on language alone. I wish we could at least video call. Once I became an operative, I'd get a smartphone. I hoped Clay would some day, as well. "As much as anyone can."

"That's the scary part," he said, "but remember, they were scholars. We're fighters. We can defend ourselves." I didn't like the certainty in his voice.

"They were trained, too, Clay. Maybe not just in fighting, but they weren't without defenses."

I had no clue what those defenses had been, and wished I'd have asked a few more questions at the briefing.

"Ya, but still—a bunch of scholars with their noses in books," I could practically hear his shrug.

"So, we'd get slaughtered less fast? I mean, we have to be careful, Clay. That's all I'm saying."

"I get that," he said, some of the brashness tempered from his voice, though I hoped it wasn't just for my benefit. "Listen, Tira," he said, a slight hesitation in his voice. I sat up straighter. Clay rarely hesitated. When he did, it was usually because he knew I'd get mad.

"Are you sure the Guild of Shadows isn't behind this?"

I choked out a laugh. "Behind the slaughter? Clay! Come on, you know we didn't do this!"

"Not you!" he said quickly. "But, like, your Guild isn't good. It kills people, Tira."

"So does yours!" I tried to keep my voice level. This argument was not only tired, it also just kept getting more and more annoying. And it was worse knowing my Guild was listening. Clay wasn't an idiot—he realized they would be. Why the hell was he putting me in this position?

"Just people who step in the arena," he said, an edge to his voice.

"Like me?" I snapped back, referring to his Boss throwing me in there as a punishment.

"You didn't die," he said sheepishly.

"But you did," I finished softly. He'd died, kind of, because Ian had poisoned him. Kept him down, quiet, until he could be revived. To give himself a chance to pull me out. But the sight of Clay falling, turning sickly gray, not moving, my screams echoing in my head…I closed my eyes, took a deep breath.

"I'm okay," he said, as though sensing my angst over the phone. Which he probably could. Clay could be thick, but he knew me. He was my best friend, and looked out for me, in a way no one else did. Just like I did for him, which was why we were both worried for one another.

What else could we be?

"I wish we were together," I said softly.

"Me, too."

"Be careful."

"You, too." He paused, "we'll meet up again soon, 'kay?"

"Sure," I said, feeling the weight of his distance pressing down on my chest. He was only a few minutes away, but he might as well be across the world.

"Maybe I'll come your way." I smiled at that thought. But I knew he wouldn't. I'd have to go to him. And I would, again and again, as often as necessary, to see him.

"Sure," I said again. "See you soon."

He repeated the same words to me, but they felt empty. We hung up, and I felt no better for having chatted with him. I mean, I felt better knowing he was alive, sure. But the rift between Clay and I seemed to be growing, and it wasn't just physical anymore.

I hoped he was right, and that we'd see each other

soon. Being friends with Clay had been easier when he was right there, and my only friend.

That realization made me feel much worse.

"We've got a mission," Ian's voice made me jump.

"How long have you been standing there?" I asked, a bit more of an edge to my voice than I'd intended. It's not like I didn't know that I'd be watched.

"Do you want to come?" He ignored my question.

"Wait. You want to bring me on a mission?" I stood up, fatigue lifted by the thought of getting out into the field and doing something useful.

"It's not super exciting," Ian said, "but I think you're ready for a test outside of the Guild." He narrowed his eyes. "Don't make me regret this, Tira."

"I won't," I grinned at him. "This is exciting!"

"It won't be, but don't screw it up anyway," he said darkly. I smiled even more widely.

I didn't care if it was exciting or not. I needed some fresh air, and a change of venue.

Anywhere not here was bound to be more exciting.

4

THE CITY'S perfume filled my lungs: fast food and cars, sequins and leather, fears and hope.

I'd missed this. This Guild of Shadows outpost, a temporary one from what I'd been told, stood at the edge of several interesting and diverse neighborhoods. I really wanted to visit them more, but I didn't exactly have an all-access pass to the outside.

This would have to do.

"Hide us," Ian instructed as he walked beside me. I grinned. I hadn't been able to fold my shadows for over a month, encouraged to learn new skills beyond my vanishing act.

There were three other initiates with us, including Rachel. I grinned at her. I was glad she was here.

I'd never folded my shadows over so many people and indicated with a quick movement of my hand for them to get closer to me. They obliged, though a few of them looked uncomfortable and confused.

It was nighttime. There were few lights, and plenty of shadows danced beyond their boundaries. I pulled them as tightly as I could, folding them around us until we vanished. I didn't feel as successful as usual.

I squinted and stopped.

"One second," I said, and closed my eyes. I reached out more deeply. Not just to the surface of the shadows, the ones cast with sharp edges to the light, but to the shadows hidden in eternal corners, unwilling to ever bend to the light. Holding ground, refusing to let it go, shadows cast centuries ago when stones were set and buildings erected.

No, the city wasn't old enough. The shadows were maybe a hundred years old, and deep, piercing, wizened. They were slow and sluggish, unwilling to move to my whim. Comfortable in their corners, in their homes, they stayed put and didn't heed my call.

I reopened my eyes. The shadows were still folded around all five of us, but not as thickly as I wanted them to be. On close observation, we would be revealed.

"It's good enough for where we're going," Ian said.

I nodded. He'd been testing me, to see how much my shadows could stretch effectively. I suppose it was better to test it now than in a battle situation.

"What are we going to do, anyway?" I whispered. My shadows didn't hide sound.

"Let's get there, first," he said, not unkindly, and led us down a second dark alleyway. Rats scurried by, feasting on garbage that was waiting for a pickup that never came. Not a soul lurked in sight, which I found distracting. Had they cleared the alleyway before we left the Guild of Shadows?

"Okay, concentrate," Ian whispered, squeezing my upper arm, making it clear he spoke to me. And I could see why. The alleyway gave way to a busy, well-lit street. I knew that street, and my heart skipped a beat. I used to come here with Clay, after capers, and we'd watch people go by. Well, I would. Clay would usually be thinking about the battle we'd just had, or the one we'd head into next. Knowing him, that's what I imagine he'd been doing, anyway.

But not me. I loved watching the people go by, living their lives. Their outfits all color and shine, and their shoes! So far outside the realm of my usual black outfit and combat boots.

And how confidently they walked in the light. I mean, they were all human, but still, they owned their space so freely! Wearing patterns and big hair like a shield against the night.

"We need to get on the other side of the street," Ian said, "without being seen."

"I don't think I can do that," I said, looking at the

well-lit street, cars slowly going by, pedestrians flashing down the sidewalk. It was busy, and bright.

So very bright.

"Maybe if I take one of us at a time?" I offered.

Ian shook his head. "No, we need to see how far we can push your shadows. Don't shy away from this test."

"I hate tests," I mumbled.

"I know," he said matter-of-factly, but a smile tugged at his lips before he looked away.

I'm glad one of us is enjoying this.

Everyone gathered around me. Rachel looked supportive, though I could tell she really had no clue what the hell I was doing.

Well, that was fine, because neither did I.

I glared at the light as I pulled the shadows to me— from the alley surrounding us, from the cracks in the pavement and the holes between the bricks. From under scurrying rats and our own feet.

It wasn't enough.

I took a deep breath, reaching further. I could sense the shadows all around me. They comforted me in a way that nothing else could, not even Clay. They promised safety, and warmth, and acceptance. And, more importantly, they promised invisibility. To keep prying eyes from my purple skin and devil horns. From my differences, so piercing, so noticeable, so judgment-worthy.

I appealed to them to cover my friends, some of

whom looked human but others who were unmistakably Traded, too. To keep us safe. To welcome us into their fold.

The shadows thickened around me. Like a veil throbbing with energy and anxiety, with my fears and worries, with my need to get them across a street.

The shadows lightened again.

"Damn it," I muttered, trying to call them back. But my hold was tenuous, and I knew it. Sweat slid down the side of my face.

"Stay close," my voice strained in my ears.

I started walking. It was now or never.

The others stayed close. Rachel and Ian were the closest. A tall man whose name I didn't know was behind me. A shorter woman walked beside him.

I really had to get better at remembering names.

As I thought this, the shadows lost some of their density.

Damn it.

We neared the light.

Almost there...

The darkness ended abruptly just a few steps ahead, a streetlight slicing it away.

I took another step, focused intently on keeping the shadows around me. They throbbed with impatience, wanting to retreat back to their natural habitat, afraid of the light.

Stay, I commanded.

I imagined tucking them near me, like a comforting blanket. They fought me a bit less.

At least, until the next step, when they pulsated around me, as afraid of the light as I was. A headache sliced through my brain. I winced and stared at the light.

Just one more step ahead of me.

I can do this. I can keep everyone hidden.

But the other side of the street seemed ridiculously far. It wasn't, I knew on a practical level. Only maybe fifteen steps. The road wasn't even double-laned. But there were a lot of people, and so much light...

A man walked by, thigh-high boots glittering with multi-colored gemstones, and the shadows vanished. No warning. Not even a chance to hold them back.

I gasped.

"Scatter," Ian said, and pulled me back into thicker shadows.

I barely noticed, so stunned by my inability to keep the shadows wrapped around me.

By the time I focused again, we had ducked back into a small alley, and only Ian remained.

"Where did the others go?" I asked, my voice weak. I tried (rather unsuccessfully) to hide my embarrassment.

"They've gone to their posts."

"They didn't need my help to cross the street." A test. I thought the test would be of my fighting abilities or my stealth skills. Well, I supposed it had been about stealth.

"No," he said. "But you needed their help to see how far you could push your shadows."

"I couldn't do it," I whispered. I looked into the shadows around us. They seemed to retreat from me, staying just outside my grasp. Like I'd scared them by forcing them. I'd never felt them shy away from me like that before. Ignored me, sure. Even turned against me. But never feared me.

I hated it.

"You okay?" Ian asked, not like an instructor, or the second-in-command of the Guild, but like a friend. It had been a while since I'd seen that Ian.

"I miss my friend," I said.

"You can't go off to see Clay tonight."

"No, I meant you."

"Oh," realization dawned on him. He gave me an apologetic smile. "Sorry. But I must train you and the others, first. It's my job."

"It's more important than friendship?" I said, half-asking, half-not. I wasn't sure I wanted to know, but feared that maybe I already did.

"I don't think so," he said, more softly. "I just want to push you to stay safe."

"Sounds like something a friend would do," I said more to myself than him, feeling better. Momentarily. "Why can't I keep the shadows wrapped around me?"

Ian seemed to ponder it for a few moments. "Do you like the other initiates who were with us?"

"I don't know two of their names," I shrugged.

His eyebrows shot up. "You've been training with them for three months."

"I don't need to know names to give and avoid blows, Ian."

"I guess not," he said, though I felt I'd disappointed him. Well, he could join the club. He redirected the line of questioning. "Did you find it difficult to stretch your shadows across two people before?"

"It's definitely tougher," I said. "So, I guess five is too many?"

"Mmmmm," Ian said, non-committal.

"I guess it's back to the Guild for me," I said softly, pondering for a few moments if I could escape and go meet up with Clay. But Ian could change into a wolf and stop me, and chances were that the Guild would come after me.

"That was a test, Tira, not the mission," Ian said, observing me closely, as though expecting me to explode or run.

I wasn't sure I wouldn't do either of those things yet, either. "It wasn't?"

"No," he offered. "There's another research guild not far from us. We need to keep an eye on it. Hopefully spot trouble before it hits."

"Oh," I said. "I guess that makes sense. Are we

expecting another hit?" I looked at Ian. "Oh," it dawned on me. "Another one's already been hit."

"Whatever this is, it's moving quickly, and seems to be targeting the research guilds."

"Can't we evacuate them?" I asked.

Ian sighed, a rare sound of frustration. "Guilds can't just…move," he said. "There are deals in place with the Watch."

"The Watch?" I asked. That sounded pretty cool, and ominous at the same time.

"Just keep an eye on the guild," Ian said, pressing a square device in my palm. It was a weird-looking, really thing smartphone. A map glowed on it, marking a building across the street. I guessed that was the Guild. I clicked on it, and some information came up.

"It's coded to you specifically," Ian said, "and the chips will fuse if it's separated from you. So, no dying trying to protect information."

I nodded, not about to admit that I wasn't about to die for Guild secrets. Not these ones, anyway.

"This," he indicated a button, "will monitor your vitals. If they spike, or you're injured, we'll know, and come help. If you need help, you press it twice for immediate evac or assistance. Understood?"

"Straightforward enough," I mumbled. "How big are the chances that we'll get in trouble?"

"Stay in the shadows. Don't let the guild even know

you're there. If it's attacked, don't engage. Just signal us."

"Pretty good then."

"This is the guild closest to ours, so operatives will move more quickly to help. We're rotating the teams so some are getting sleep right now. We need initiates to be our eyes, so the operatives can be combat-ready."

"And the other initiates?" I was thinking of Rachel, and her explosive tendencies.

"Same," he said. "Just keeping an eye out on other guilds."

"How many are near?" I asked.

He ignored my question. "There are operatives close to every guild. But to always be watching carefully and then be full focus for combat is a lot to ask of anyone, and is sure to get our people killed. We need to split the work."

"Okay."

"Okay," he replied, though his eyebrow raised a bit as though he didn't believe I'd stay out of trouble.

"Be careful," he said, and began to walk back toward the Guild of Shadows.

"Wait!" I asked. "What about you?"

He gave me a slight smile. "I need some sleep."

I suddenly realized how tired and haggard he looked. He'd probably been on high alert since the Rosetta Guild had been hit.

"Be careful," I said for good measure. He nodded,

seemed about to tell me the same, but realized he'd already said it several times. He turned and vanished around a corner.

I focused back on the street. According to the info on my smartphone, there was a good observation point from the top of the Galileo Guild, which occupied the top two floors of a nearby six-story building.

Light blanketed the entire street ahead. And I didn't want to pester the shadows again, skittish at the edges of my power. I had a job to do, which was exciting! But I had to cross the light to do it, which was annoying.

I sighed. No point in stretching this out.

I pulled up my hood, lowered my head, and stepped into the light.

5

"*Keep an eye out*" wasn't the most detailed and clear instruction I'd ever received. I'd never spent any time just *being* out here. How the hell was I supposed to suddenly be judge and jury of what was normal and what wasn't?

Maybe I could use that to my advantage? Go explore a bit under pretext that someone was being suspicious?

"*What were they doing, Tira?*"

"*They closed their shoe store early! That seemed suspicious.*"

"*So, you went in there?*"

"*Yes! To keep an eye out, as instructed.*"

"*Why do you suddenly have five shiny pairs of shoes?*"

No, there really was no way I'd talk my way out of that. Besides, I'd spotted two cameras already, lower on the building, which had probably been hacked by the Guild of Shadows. They hacked everything else, so why not this? As far as I could tell, they already had eyes on this building.

So why the hell am I here? Why did the Guild of Shadows need me here if they could just rely on their equipment? Unless, of course, they feared the equipment might not pick up the attackers.

I leaned against the stone barrier surrounding the roof. This must be used as some sort of patio during warmer seasons.

I glanced up. A few of the nearby buildings were slightly taller, but they looked abandoned. Or maybe just closed during the night.

I looked down at the dim green map on the screen and tapped on the building to the right. Information came up, including which businesses populated it, and a current people count, currently just two. I tapped on it, and it brought up details on two security guards, and their current positions in the building.

"Wow," I whispered.

There was a hell of a lot more I had to learn about being an operative of the Guild of Shadows.

They were certainly well connected. And yet they needed in-person surveillance, which solidified my theory that they feared not being able to detect the attackers with technology. Or, maybe they didn't fear it. Maybe they knew from experience.

I clicked on the building below me. The screen lit up: *Galileo Guild*. It focused on scientific research, but that was all the info it gave me. No list of people, floor layouts, or any other pertinent details. Maybe the guilds didn't like to share with each other.

Or maybe the guilds didn't like dealing with the Guild of Shadows...although the Rosetta Guild had fed us information. Maybe they were the exception, not the rule. I remembered Clay's warning. That the Guild of Shadows was dangerous.

To some, maybe. But weren't we all dangerous to someone? Clay thought they were dangerous to everyone, but I didn't think so. I mean, the Guild of Shadows *did* kill people, yes, but only to maintain the balance. To make sure that the Traded didn't end up in a war with humans that we couldn't win, or that wouldn't leave thousands, if not millions, dead.

But what if I was wrong? What if Ian was a bad guy? Like, a *really* bad guy?

No. I couldn't think that way. Ian had saved me. He'd almost died protecting me. He'd respected my friendship with Clay.

But...Ian was second-in-command. Ian might also be torn between the Guild and who he wanted to be.

We all had our part to play, after all. That was hammered into our heads time and time again, since going to the Academy, and now at the Guild. All of us are part of a great machine, a cog in the universe.

Except the Traded had been thrown into the human machine to sabotage it. Could we learn to work within it, or would we bring it to a grinding halt?

We all must respect the part we must play.

Shit. This was so boring, I was going to introspect myself to dust.

Why the hell am I here?

I looked back at my screen, empty of pertinent information on the guild below.

Because I can get in there, and they don't have information. What if Ian couldn't actually ask me to do this, so he'd have plausible deniability? What if they really needed intel, and just couldn't afford for one of their full-fledged operatives to be caught?

Whereas an initiate with a track record of sneaking away and not being the best at listening to instructions...well, that could be explained.

Maybe that was the test. Could I independently see what needed to be done and just do it? Get the work done without being caught or stopped? Could my judgement be trusted?

A siren sounded in the distance, its origin lost as it bounced off the nearby buildings, shadows gently pulsing around me.

I realized that I'd folded into them without even noticing. They'd easily come to me, let me hide in them, didn't shy away from my touch. I reached out and stroked them, smiling.

I'd scared the shadows in the alley by pushing them too far. They'd come back now, understanding that I only tried to work with them, and make them better.

Maybe Ian was doing the same thing. I'd gotten complacent at the Guild. Hell, I hadn't even tried to sneak out lately! Maybe the test was just that: for me to push myself.

I grinned. I liked that idea. I could use something a bit more exciting, anyway, or the operatives wouldn't be the only ones catching up on their sleep tonight.

Comforted by the shadows around me and the silence that blanketed the alley, I hopped over the stone guard, grabbed a pipe that ran up, planted my feet, and dangled my body over the edge to find an easy access point to the Galileo Guild.

Oh, this was going to be fun. Just below, maybe two stories down, a balcony kindly greeted me. One of the best parts about being in the Guild of Shadows was the fun gear. I touched the back of my belt, pulling free the three prongs that made the end of my grappling hook, the thin but resistant rope coiled inside my belt.

I hooked it to the venting pipe and rappelled down. Damn, that was fun. Much better than the jumps Clay and I used to take. Painful on even Traded knees and not super subtle, either.

I nudged the grappling hook free as soon as I found my footing, keeping the shadows tight around me. The balcony gave way to a double glass door. Both doors were opened, thick red curtains slightly parting to let in the air.

This place doesn't exactly feel super secure.

It was probably a good thing that I was sneaking in here. It was ripe for attack!

I checked on my shadows, still feeling a bit nervous about them deserting me in the alley. But they seemed content around me, carrying the light scent of wood and books wafting from within the Guild.

Huh. I guess that made sense for a researchers' guild, though I expected more computers nowadays, and fewer books.

I carefully approached the opening between the curtains, which revealed dim lights within.

Pushing the curtains aside I slipped in quietly, the shadows thick around me. I stopped, cocked my head, and listened.

All was quiet.

I took another step.

"Um, hi," a granular voice said. I turned around, eyes wide, at the person looking at me, despite my folded shadows.

So much for not being spotted.

6

"Hɪ," I replied, so as not to be completely rude. I mean, I was already sneaking in, but still. I spotted a figure between two bookshelves, in shadows so deep even I couldn't make out his features.

Ian wouldn't be super happy to know I'd been spotted so easily. Or at all.

Candles flickered around the room, creating the light, though they were the LED kind, not the fire kind. Smart, considering the stacks of papers and books surrounding them.

"Are you here to slaughter us?" the granular voice asked.

"Um, no," I answered. "I'm here to help keep an eye out."

"Great!" he didn't take a step forward, staying ensconced in the shadows. But I'd started to make him out, bandages covering most of his skin, his flopped ears obviously not human, his green glowing eyes focused on me. "Will sneaking through a window keep us safe?"

"Just having a look around," I mumbled, my tail swishing in annoyance behind me. I hated when it did that. It didn't seem to escape the mummy's attention, though he was wise enough not to mention it.

He seemed to weigh my words, and then motioned to the room around him, not fully extending his arms, as though he feared leaving his body unprotected. I noticed his hunch, too. He just generally looked uncomfortable, like pain lanced his entire body with unseen needle pricks.

"This is the library," he said, his voice also grated with pain. "Well, one of them. We mostly just have libraries here."

"Are you okay?" I asked, taking a step toward him. He shuffled back and I stopped, holding out my hands. "It's okay. I won't hurt you."

He flinched and stared at me with those unblinking green eyes. "Okay."

I debated what to ask next. I'd never met anyone from a research guild before! Not too surprising, considering I hadn't even known that they existed until today. Still! I bet he knew and saw a bunch of cool stuff. I wondered what exactly they were researching.

"How come you see me?" I asked, realizing I still held the shadows against me.

"Shiny eyes," he grinned.

"They are very shiny," I offered. He nodded. His teeth were either green or reflected his eyes. That was unclear. I'd expected them to be sharpened, but they were quite human looking, aside from the color.

I dropped my shadows just as a *thunk* caught my attention. Both the mummy and I glanced toward the door, which stood open past three tables covered in books, flanked by tall bookshelves that reached up to the dark, tall ceiling.

I motioned to him to stay there, but I doubted he would have moved anyway. He seemed to have withdrawn even more, folding into himself.

Pulling free my new favorite toy, a sleek, long handgun that had both taser and laser-cutting action, I headed to the door. A strangled cry resonated down the hall, before cutting off abruptly.

I pulled out my smartphone and hit every button at least three times and headed down the corridor, gun before me, and folding my shadows around me like a protective armor. It would be nice if they *could* block a blow, and not just visibility.

I hoped the intruder didn't also have shiny eyes.

7

DESPITE SPENDING the last three months in training, I felt rustier than I ever had on missions with Clay. We hadn't even had any training—we were just having fun pulling off heists and doing random jobs. I mean, we'd had battle and skills training, sure, to be useful to the guilds, but we hadn't had sneaking out training.

That would have been entirely too useful.

But now, after being trained for specific missions like this for the past three months, and after spending years looking forward to my next escape with Clay, I felt completely out of my element.

I guess I wasn't used to being out here, alone. Also, "find the shiny object" was way more fun than "try not to get sliced in two."

I preferred the former, by far.

The carpet absorbed my footsteps, but I still walked

carefully, in case a creaky floorboard lurked beneath the padded surface. The walls were drywall. Stone or metal would be more comforting. Drywall did nothing to stop bullets or sharp claws.

My eyes wandered from detail to detail, trying to capture everything. Anything could be a trap, or an important signal of danger. My mind whirled with possibilities, mostly of what could go wrong.

Most scenarios ended with me being sliced in two.

Well, that was my problem. The Guild had taught me to think, and thinking too much on these missions just slowed me down. I took a deep breath, focused on the corridor, the here and now, and took another step forward.

A door emerged to the left, partly closed, light escaping into the corridor. Blood dribbled lazily into the carpet, absorbing at its edge.

Well, shit.

I wished Clay were here. Or Ian. Or Rachel. Someone to watch my back. I'd rarely been on missions by myself.

I wasn't a fan.

The blood stained deep red on the cream carpet, so it might be human. I held my weapon before me, images of the slaughter flashing before my mind's eye.

I took a deep breath, forced them down. *What happened can't be changed, Tira, so focus on turning what might be into what should be.*

Like me getting out with all my body parts.

I heard a slight scraping behind me, and I whipped around. Several people, looking terrified and about my age, headed my way. I dropped the shadows and held up my hand, to indicate I wasn't the enemy, while gesturing for them to be quiet.

Thankfully, none of them screamed. And they stopped. I nodded and indicated the door where I'd left the mummy behind. One, I guess their leader, shook her head and pointed to the end of the corridor.

I spotted the stair access at the end of it.

There was no way in hell I could get them all out safely. I couldn't wrap my shadows around all of them, I was sure of that. We might be seen anyway, as the mummy had proved. Or someone would make noise, and we'd be detected.

Too risky.

They just had to cover twenty feet to reach the stairs, but it might as well be a hundred miles. I shook my head and indicated the pooling blood. The leader blanched and herded her friends into the room near them. They were thankfully quiet. Then again, they were probably trained to be quiet in libraries.

I turned back to the door, ready to at least see what the intruders looked like. Who the hell had done so much damage, so quickly and effectively? Part of me was impressed, sure, but a bigger part of me liked the idea of surviving. I didn't intend to get in a fight with them if I could avoid it.

I folded my shadows back around me, drawing them from every nook and cranny, every crack and carpet fiber, to shield me against sight.

I took a deep breath, careful to remain silent, and peeked around the corner. Blood dribbled lazily from the multiple wounds in the Traded's body, but I didn't allow my gaze to linger on her.

I stepped over her, careful not to get blood on my boots. I felt a pang at her glassy eyes, my mind demanding answers as to who she was, what she loved, what her dreams had been...

Focus.

Something dangerous lurked here, and enough people could see through my shadows that I really had no guarantees that I wouldn't be spotted.

The room's dim light gifted me with more shadows, the few lamps knocked over. In the shadows, I could see more bodies. I heard a muffled moan.

I clutched my gun, held it before me and steadied it with my other hand. I scanned my surroundings, keeping my back to the door. There was only one way out of the room. The whole place smelled of... cookies? Sugar? Something sweet.

It wasn't a kitchen though. Shelves guarded the walls, brimming with stark, thick gray folders. Blood splatters covered the few worktables. I crouched to scan beneath the tables, in case an attacker hid there.

Thunk.

I whipped up, tightening my shadows around me, my breath coming faster. I could smell sugar again. I froze, trying to figure out its origin.

Someone screamed. Quick. Sharp. Terrified.

Surprised.

Then stopped.

It came from down the hall, where I'd left the other Traded.

Shit.

I ran back, slowing down as I reached the closed door. How had they gotten in? Maybe I'd been wrong and I'd just heard someone stumbling?

I gently turned the handle and pushed the door open, slipping in and quickly moving to the side, shadows tightly wrapped around me. I looked around, eyes wide.

What the hell...

Bodies. A pile of them, slashed and bleeding, some in pieces. I'd left them for barely a minute. And nothing had gotten past me!

I ignored the blank, staring eyes, looked carefully around me. I couldn't see anything, or anyone. But obviously something was here.

The door had still been closed.

Something moved to my left, between two

bookshelves. I crouched, springing toward the movement, pulling out a dagger.

"Wait," the whisper came. Glowing green eyes pleaded with me. I steadied my hand, put my back against the wall, and squinted at him.

"Did you do this?"

He looked shocked at the question, then seemed to ponder it.

"No," he answered, his voice wavering. His bandages weren't covered in blood, nor was he wounded. Besides, he'd been in this room when the slaughter had occurred in the next room.

But how had they, or *it*, gotten in?

"Let's get out of here," I whispered, and wrapped my shadows around him. With any luck, the creature, or whatever the hell the thing was, couldn't see through them.

I walked around the table and nudged him along, but he hesitated, not moving from his spot.

"I don't think I can walk," he whispered, and pointed to his leg. I looked down, and half of his right leg was missing, a lazy string of...not blood, but goo dribbling beneath it.

"It'll heal," he shrugged.

"Okay," I stared down, the dark liquid not leaking but gelling together, almost like it was trying to form another limb. A loose, viscous limb, dangling there.

Gross.

Another thump, near the window. I helped my weird friend back into his hiding spot, indicated he should be quiet. He nodded and crouched, carefully folding his missing limb so as not to touch the wounded portion. I stood over him, my shadows still stretched over both of us, and grabbed my gun and my dagger.

A few shadows slipped in quietly through the window. I never thought I'd feel such relief at seeing the Guild of Shadows. I hesitated for half a second and dropped my shadows.

Ian looked surprised for half a second, before turning angry.

I guess disobeying orders hadn't been my test, after all.

I indicated to the still-breathing researcher. The mummy gave Ian a little shy wave.

Ian composed himself and nodded. He motioned to two other operatives, and in an instant they were carrying the Traded out the window. He didn't make a noise. Either the mummy had a great resistance to pain, or he didn't feel any.

I turned to Ian, who raised an eyebrow. I shrugged and looked around, my eyes a bit wider than they should be.

He held up his hand and put up one finger, indicating the bodies and then everything around.

I shrugged again and shook my head. I didn't know

if the attackers were still here, because I didn't know how they'd gotten past me in the first place.

I apparently managed to convey something that made sense to Ian, since he nodded. Two more operatives entered the room. I wondered if others had accessed via different entry points.

Ian looked at me and pointed back out the window. I shook my head. Like hell I was leaving. They might need me. My shadows might keep someone safe.

Besides, I'd told these people to hide here, and they'd all died. I had to do something to help.

So I wouldn't feel as shitty about all of this.

I straightened my back and my hands turned to fists at my side. Ian's eyes narrowed as he studied me, then he nodded. He motioned for an operative to follow him down the hall, and motioned for me and the other operative, a Traded I didn't recognize, to head back towards the room with the previous slaughter.

I hated that Ian had sent me the one way he figured I'd be safe. I hated even more that he was probably heading towards the attackers.

The corridor ahead stood silent, but that hardly meant anything. I drew my shadows around me. The other Guild of Shadows operative walked ahead to scout, out of reach of my shadows.

Which was fine—the chances of an attack here were slim. I glanced back. Ian and the other operative were already gone. I hadn't even heard them open a door to slip into. Mind you, I had no clue what the other operative could do, and Ian might be a mouse by now.

The operative turned into the room. I followed, disinterested, until I heard a weird noise, like a *squick*.

The operative flew back out the door in several pieces, landing hard against the wall, blood exploding all over the hallway.

I shifted sideways, halfway through pulling out my dagger, when the air beside me shimmered in my folded shadows. I freed my blade and struck hard, a shriek echoing in my skull, my body flying, blood, a thump…*shit.*

Was that me?

8

I KNEW I wasn't dead because being dead wouldn't hurt this bad. Breathing wouldn't burn my chest. Stars wouldn't be going supernova before my eyes.

I dragged my shadows around me, folding them tightly. I hadn't seen the creature, until it had crossed them. That meant it couldn't see me if I kept to my shadows, as long as it didn't run into me.

With any luck, it was long gone by now.

Ian!

He'd be heading back here. I didn't think I'd screamed, but the creature certainly had. I might have, too. I wasn't sure.

Another shallow breath.

Blood.

I could taste blood. I struggled to stay conscious, to

hold my shadows around me. But I had to help the others, too.

Ian.

I pushed myself onto my elbows, or at least tried. I went back down quickly. I couldn't breathe. Try as I might, I couldn't get breath in fully, and blood kept getting in my way. I choked on the thick liquid in my throat and spit some out, my sight still uncooperative, my hands unwilling to move, my shadows slipping away from me...I tried to hold them, but I couldn't breathe.

I couldn't breathe, and I couldn't see.

Darkness lifted the light from my eyes and I thought I heard someone calling my name.

Maybe the Traded get to go home when they die.

The thought warmed me, and I dropped my shadows and slipped away into the darker shadows awaiting at the edge of my consciousness.

"Tira!"

THE FLOOR SHIFTED AND MOVED. Pain lanced my side. My chest. My heart.

I gasped, moaned.

Slipped away.

~

"TIRA."

Clay?

Was Clay here? He couldn't be here. He'd get hurt.

I tried to open my eyes, but couldn't, like something thick held them closed.

"Shh, be quiet."

It wasn't Clay. But it was a friend.

I tried to cling to consciousness. It was important that I stay awake. To stay safe. To warn my friends.

Ian!

The adrenaline rush pushed light before my eyes and vanquished my breath.

~

"FIVE MORE," a voice said. I didn't know them.

I tried to move.

"Don't move," another voice said. *Ian.* I knew that voice.

I stopped moving.

I managed to open my left eye a bit, enough for the light to sting. A tear escaped the edge of my eyelid as the shape before me formed into Ian.

Covered in blood.

"My blood?" I wanted to ask, but just gurgled.

His hands came up to my forehead. The warmth comforted me. "Shh. You're safe now. Rest."

How do you know we're safe? I wanted to ask, but couldn't.

I already knew the answer anyway. He didn't know if we were safe. He couldn't know.

He just hoped damn hard that we were.

9

———————————

I WOKE up to the soft hum of a machine. I opened my eyes slowly, pleased that they weren't crusty and that I could focus.

A drip machine stood guard beside me, regularly sighing a clear liquid down the tube hooked to the needle in my arm. My purple skin looked a bit gray, my gut hurt, and I was parched.

And all of that was fine. Because, hell, it meant I was still alive.

What a day, I thought as I looked around. I was in the infirmary, the other beds distressingly empty. A curtain separated me from the bed right next door. Two glowing orbs shone through them.

I blinked, making sure it wasn't a trick of the light or my tired eyes.

"Hello?" I said, my voice raw.

"Hi," the voice replied, the two orbs moving to the side of the curtain to peek around them. The mummified researcher's head peeked at me with unblinking eyes. "I'm glad you're okay."

"Thanks," I said. "I'm glad you're okay, too."

He grinned, his teeth picking up some of the green from his eyes. Not a super restful sight.

"Was anyone else hurt?" I asked, my voice small. I thought I remembered Ian bringing me to safety, but the memories were fuzzy from pain...and almost dying.

His head cocked sideway slowly. Damn, I wish he'd blink. "Everyone from my guild is dead," he grinned again, "except me."

"Yes," I tried not to let impatience drip into my voice. It didn't seem fair to take out my worries on him, though I wasn't sure he'd actually notice. "What about from *my* Guild?"

"Oh." He seemed to ponder for a bit. "I don't know."

"Okay."

I stared at the ceiling. How badly hurt was I? I tried to push myself up, but something pulled at my stomach. Pain ripped through my gut, stars exploded in front of my eyes, and I laid back down, winded and hurting.

Pretty badly hurt.

I healed fast. Most Traded did. But this would take a while, and a killer was out there.

"You got sliced up pretty bad," the voice said. I

turned my head and started at the two glowing eyes, now much closer.

"Please don't do that." I said. He stood right beside me, crouched so his head hovered near mine.

"Don't do what?" He sounded honestly perplexed.

"Your leg!" I asked, wanting to look down but not daring to move.

"I don't know how not to do my leg," he offered.

"What? No! I mean…your leg. It's okay?"

"It grew back," he said with a grin, holding it up so I could see it, though it was mostly hidden beneath thick robes.

"Nice," I said, and meant it. That was a pretty useful trait. "How long have I been out?" It seemed a nicer question than "how long does it take to grow back a leg?"

"About a day?" he said. Followed by another puzzled look. "I don't know."

"You've been in here two days," Ian said, his voice soft as he stepped into the room. I felt immediate relief at seeing him. My breathing eased. I hadn't even realized how I'd been holding my breath with worry.

He squeezed my shoulder and looked up to the mummy. "You have a room," he offered. "You don't have to stay in the infirmary now that you've been discharged."

The mummy hesitated, then nodded. "I'm glad you're okay," he said, and shuffled off.

Ian watched him go. "Well, at least we saved one from the Galileo Guild," he looked back my way. It kind of sounded like he was thanking me, but it also kind of sounded like a reprimand. That was a good trick.

"No one else from the Guild of Shadows got hurt, except Tim. There was nothing we could do for him."

I nodded. I mean, I felt bad that he'd died, but I didn't even know who Tim was. Maybe I should put more effort into getting to know the people here. Or, then again, maybe not, if they were all going to get disemboweled in front of me.

"Did you see the creature?" I asked, my voice annoyingly weak.

He shook his head. "No, but you hurt it with your dagger. We found a trail of blood leading all the way out of the building, but then we lost the trail."

"What kind of blood?" I asked, wishing I could sit up.

"Well, not human. We couldn't even detect it without a UV light."

"Huh."

"You were hurt bad, Tira," Ian said softly.

"I'll be okay."

"But you might not have been," he said. "We've lost so many Traded, and we'll just keep losing more unless we stop this thing, whatever it is." His frustration dissipated into a question. "How did you manage to hit it, anyway?"

"When it crossed my shadows," I said, remembering the strange ripple, "it made some kind of trail."

Ian considered my words, his eyes growing darker. I wanted to reach up and touch his face, just to connect with someone. But moving my arm seemed impossible, and my eyelids grew heavy.

"Sleep," he said as I lost the battle to keep my eyes open. "We have a big day ahead."

I thought I felt his lips on my forehead as I drifted off, but it might have just been his hand, speeding me toward welcoming dreams.

I WOKE UP WITH A START, gurgling out a tired scream as someone held me down.

"Tira," someone said. I didn't know their voice. I didn't know them, and they were holding me down, and I needed to be free. I needed to call my shadows to me.

"We can't help her if we can't see her," someone else said, sounding annoyed.

"Tira," the voice spoke right beside my ear, warm breath grounding.

Ian.

"Lie still. You're in no danger, I promise you. They'll heal you."

I tried to open my eyes but felt myself gently drift away.

"I promise I won't leave you," he said. I believed him and allowed myself to fall prey to sleep once more, confident that I wouldn't be alone.

That I was safe.

10

"HI," the sing-song voice chanted beside me the second I stirred awake.

I opened my eyes to the sight of two glowing green eyes right beside me. I blinked, too tired to start.

Pain no longer coiled my abdomen, and moving my arms proved easier. I placed my forefinger in the middle of the mummy's forehead and gently pushed him back, his strange grin unchanging.

"Space, please," I said.

He cocked his head a bit as though considering it, and then shuffled back a few more steps. He seemed stiff, like he'd been crouching beside me too long.

"How long have you been...you know what, never mind. What can I do for you?"

"I had breakfast," he said, looking pleased. "And I thought I'd see if you'd like breakfast, too." He looked to the side table, his grin unwavering. A platter of congealed eggs sat there.

I now knew how long he'd been here: too long.

The mummy opened his mouth, closed it, then pointed down to the end of my bed. "I like your puppy," he said. I glanced down. Ian was there in the dog form that he'd been in when we'd first met. He looked groggy and annoyed.

I'd never been happier to see his grumpy, fuzzy face. I realized it had been months since I'd seen his dog form, and I'd missed it.

I smiled at him. "You stayed," I whispered, the threads of the nightly healing returning to me. His doggie eyes had so much depth as they held mine. I patted his head, and he wagged his tail.

I liked puppy Ian. I used to call him Max, because that seemed a good dog name, but that didn't work for him anymore. I couldn't *not* see Ian in his eyes, no matter which shape he took. Well, except maybe if he became a snail.

But I'd never seen him take that particular form. Which was more than okay with me. I'd stepped on a snail once and heard its shell explode under my foot, and had already suffered several nightmares of accidentally doing that to Ian.

I shuddered at the thought.

"Okay, time to get up," I said, gently testing my abdomen. Ian jumped off the bed, making no attempt at stopping me.

I remembered a few events from the night. They'd taken out my drip, and then someone had come in and gently placed their warm hands on me. I'd drifted for a while, completely comfortable. Ian had been near. I kind of remembered him jumping onto the end of my bed.

It was a comforting weight. I'd missed it. But Ian was busy helping to run this place, so being a puppy at my feet while I slept wasn't in the cards. Maybe I needed to get an actual dog. Would the Guild of Shadows let me do that? Where would I walk the dog?

Ian cocked his head, looking at me skeptically. I was glad he couldn't read minds. At least, I was pretty sure he couldn't. I looked to the mummy. His head was also cocked, grin still frozen on his face.

I sighed. "Um, I'm sorry, what's your name?"

"Glitter," he said, pointing to his eyes.

"That's a nice name," I offered. He cocked his head further and took a step forward.

"Tira," I said. "Tira Misu."

His grin slowly faded, his eyes widened, his mouth turning into a perfect "o."

"You're a dessert!" His voice sounded a tad too thrilled.

"Just the name."

I swung my legs over the edge of the bed. I wore a boring blue hospital gown. Ian moved behind some curtains, where I assumed he was shifting. He shifted in front of me, but didn't seem like doing it in front of just anyone.

He stepped back out, the mummy giving him a look of enthusiastic wonder. Ian scowled at him and stayed close to me as I tested my legs, leaving me my space, but ready to assist if necessary. I felt the mummy, I mean Glitter, stand at my other side, also ready to help.

I stood up fully, no pain shearing my gut. My legs felt a bit shaky, but I'd been lying down for two days, so that wasn't unexpected.

"Are you sure you're all right?" Ian asked.

"Seem to be," I grinned at him, though I didn't hop around to test that statement. There would be time for that yet.

"You almost got cut in two," Glitter said.

I raised an eyebrow and stared at him.

A tentative smile popped up on his face. He looked like he was trying really hard to be friendly, but not quite hitting the mark.

"Could you give us a moment?" Ian asked Glitter.

Glitter nodded enthusiastically. And stayed there.

"I mean, alone," Ian said, his patience drawing thin.

"Oh," Glitter said. He paused, as though considering the request. I feared Ian might toss him out.

"We'll find you after, if you want to head back to your room," I offered, so he didn't feel too bad.

"Okay," he agreed and shuffled off. His back curved

in over the rest of his body. His arms folded inward, and he never really dropped them, as though the tendons were just a bit too tight. He held his head as high as he could, his neck at almost a ninety-degree angle for him to be able to look forward.

It made him look shorter than he must be, and the folding in made him look perpetually scared. Which he might be. His entire guild had just been slaughtered, after all.

"Are you sure you're all right?" Ian asked again, holding my eyes with his.

"You asked me that already," I said, then smiled gently. "And yes, I am." I placed my hand on my stomach. "Was it really as bad as Glitter said?"

"No, but nearly," he spoke softly. "Your armor took a lot of the blow and you dodged sideways, which saved you."

"I don't even remember moving," I mumbled. "I just remember hurting."

"Instincts are good," Ian said. I squinted my eyes at him.

"What?" I asked. Why had he sent Glitter away? Surely it wasn't to ask me exactly the same questions he was asking me before sending him away. Ian was hesitating, buying time for something he didn't want to do or say.

I was fine, so it wasn't about my health. Had

someone else been killed? My breath caught in my throat.

"Did Clay's league get hit?"

"No!" Ian quickly dissipated my worry. "No, I swear I wouldn't keep that from you."

"Thank you," I whispered. I didn't think Ian liked Clay. In fact, I was sure he didn't. Clay was my oldest friend, heck, my only friend, really, aside from Ian. But Clay had been so single-minded in joining a fighter's league that he'd put me in danger a few times.

Ian had taken that more personally than I had. Of course, he'd known that we wouldn't get a choice. That I'd already been marked for the Guild of Shadows, and Clay for the Wolf Pack League. So, Ian had known that all of Clay's efforts were futile.

But Clay hadn't known that. Clay had fought to keep me by his side. Even if sometimes it felt like he'd just thrown me in the path of danger, I knew Clay had done it because he cared.

For Ian, though, Clay's behavior had been selfish and dangerous. I doubted Ian had forgiven Clay, or that he ever would. Of course, Ian had no more claim on being mad on my behalf than Clay did.

And yet Clay was mad at Ian, too, because Ian had whisked me to the Guild of Shadows. More or less. I'd had to "make" the choice, but it hadn't really been a choice. Still, Clay hated my Guild and what it stood for.

He thought of it as nothing more than a league of assassins, even though I saw it as so much more.

For me, it was home.

"Have other guilds been attacked?" I asked, not really wanting to know. How many more Traded had died while I slept here?

He looked grim. "No," he said. "We wonder if your wounding the creature bought us some time."

"That would be good," I said. "You don't think it's dead?"

"We followed the trail, and it didn't seem like that much blood. Plus, the trail petered out, so it probably has healing capacities."

"The creature," I mumbled, "is probably gearing up for another attack."

"We don't know that for sure," he said even more softly, then sighed. "Look, the guilds are coming together to form a pact of some sort, to keep each other safe."

I'd have thought that was good news, but Ian looked even more irritated by it.

"That's good, right?" I asked, no longer sure.

"Of course," he said, his voice tinged with annoyance, "and we're about to meet at a neutral location," he paused, long enough for me to narrow my eyes at him. "We'd like you to report. You're the only one who's seen the creature, much less struck it."

"You want me to do what, now?" I gave an awkward

laugh. "Ian, you know I don't do spotlights, or talking in front of groups."

That was an understatement. I hated crowds. I hated being seen by so many people. I was purple. With demon horns and a tail. I belonged in the shadows.

"I know," Ian sounded annoyed, but I was pretty sure it wasn't at me. He gestured back toward the general area of Sonsil's chambers. As leader of the Guild of Shadows, Sonsil could pretty much order me to do it, no matter how much I might dislike it.

He wasn't exactly here to coddle me. It seemed no one was here to do that in this life.

"I'm not doing it," I said, but knew I could be made to do it. "Or, I'll do it while hiding in the shadows. I mean, do they really need to see me?"

Ian cocked an eyebrow. I sighed. "Look, I'm no public speaker. And I didn't see much. Besides, I already told you everything that I saw. Can't you share for me?"

I sounded pathetic, but I couldn't help my voice from dipping down. "Maybe I don't feel as good as I thought I did?" I offered hopefully.

Ian ran his hand through his disheveled hair, looked back toward the door.

"Okay, let me see what I can do," he said. "But, if you don't talk, you won't get to come."

"That's okay," I shrugged. "Sounds pretty boring anyway."

"Clay will be there," he said softly, his dark eyes locked on me, his voice too neutral to mask his true emotions. "The meeting is at his league. Fighting leagues are neutral enough, and well-defended."

I examined Ian quietly before breaking the silence. "You didn't have to tell me that."

"I know," he said, "but you'd have found out. And it's not my place to decide who your friends are." He paused, looked at me significantly. "But it is my place to make sure you stay in line with the Guild of Shadows. I trust that you won't put me in an awkward position?"

"I won't," I promised, and meant it. Just seeing Clay, for a few moments, would make the trip worthwhile. I missed him badly, about as much as I missed the shadows right now.

But I'd have to step into the light to do it, in front of Traded from different guilds, and tell them what I'd seen. What I'd felt.

Terror. That's what I'd felt. But it was nothing compared to the terror of having to stand up in front of so many people.

11

I FOUGHT the urge to fold the shadows around me as I walked back to my room. I needed to freshen up, find something to wear that wasn't a hospital gown. I looked terrible in washed-out blue.

I doubted anybody would look good in this.

I jumped a bit when Rachel stepped in front of me, her eyes the blue of the sea, her pink hair now streaked with chunks of blue, her skin shimmery like water on a sunny day.

I stood corrected. This robe would look good on her.

"Would you like this gown?" I asked. "The color would look good on you, and probably no one else."

"Um, no thank you," she said, her eyebrow slowly going up as she looked at the gown. "I'm glad you're okay."

"Thanks," I offered. "I'm gonna get changed."

"I heard you're going to the Wolf Pack League to tell them about the monster," Rachel said, not moving aside. That was all sorts of annoying, especially after offering her my gown.

"First, I have to change," I said, more than ready to elbow past her.

She opened her mouth, then closed it, apparently thinking better of it. I'd never fought Rachel in one-to-one combat. But she seemed pretty strong. Probably from years of working on a boat. I'd be curious to test my mettle with her, but feared she'd just go and explode.

That wouldn't be so great.

"Can I come chat with you after?" she asked softly.

"Um, sure, I guess."

She nodded and walked back to her room. That was weird. People didn't generally visit me. Had she missed me? That would be nice, but I doubted it. I guess I'd find out soon enough what she wanted to talk about.

I slipped into my room, the darkness comforting. I could completely vanish here, if I wanted to. I didn't need the lights and preferred them off. There was comfort in knowing not everyone could just look at you. It didn't matter that I was alone.

I tugged at my hospital gown and had it almost off when I heard someone clear their throat from beside my bed. I reached for a dagger, but of course had no weapon on me. I crouched and peered up. Two shining green eyes popped up beside the bed.

I sighed. "Glitter, what are you doing here?" The hood from his sweater covered his features.

"You said to go to my room."

"This isn't your room," I wanted nothing more than to throw him out and have a hot shower. But I couldn't bring myself to do it. The poor thing had lost his entire guild and didn't seem to know up from down.

Those two things may or may not have been related.

"No," he agreed. "It's your room."

"Then we're in agreement," I muttered. "So, you're in the wrong room."

"I don't think so," he frowned, his glowing green eyes lowering as his eyebrows stitched together. Or I imagined that's what he was doing. I couldn't see his eyebrows under all his bandages.

I realized he must have been sleeping beside my bed. Otherwise, I'd have seen the glow of his eyes right away when I walked in.

Note to self: next time, do a perimeter check of your room. Always do a perimeter check. Spare yourself having weird encounters in your own room.

"I said for you to go to *your* room." I fought to keep my voice even. "This is *my* room."

"Yes," he bopped his head up and down with

agreement, any sign of a frown line gone. "But, if I say those exact words, I'm right."

"I'm sorry?"

"Go to your room. If I'm you telling me that, I'm in the right room. This is my room." He waited for my answer, perfectly still.

"That...that doesn't make any sense."

"My room." He repeated more slowly, as though that would help me understand.

"Okay, I'm not even going to try anymore. Do you not remember where your room is?"

"Why would I forget that?"

I sighed. This was getting me nowhere, and I still wanted to shower and change into actual clothes, not to mention wrap my head around having to speak in front of a bunch of guild leaders.

My stomach rumbled, either from hunger or nerves. Maybe both.

"Well, you stay there," I said. "I'm going to grab a shower."

"Okay," he said, his eyes shifting a bit. I realized he wasn't looking *at* me, but *near* me. He couldn't see anything in the dark.

Maybe speaking to the guild leaders would turn out to be the high point of my day.

"I'm going to put the lights on for you," I said, and flipped the switch, blinking as the light burned my eyes.

"You can see in the dark," his voice held a note of wonder.

"I can also throw daggers really well in the dark," I mumbled as I grabbed clothes from my dresser.

"If you move," I said, "I will eviscerate you."

The last thing I needed was to spot two shiny green eyes through the shower glass.

"No moving," he agreed. I squinted at him. If he noticed my ire, he didn't give any indication of it.

At least he wasn't moving from there. Maybe he'd actually understood those instructions?

Not willing to take a chance, I locked the door to the bathroom before slipping under the marvellously warm stream of water.

I took my time, keeping the lights off, only the glow from my room slipping in under the bathroom door.

The scar across my abdomen was deep purple and straight, like a seam cutting me in two. I'd had other scars, though most had vanished over time, whisked away by the healing ability most Traded shared. But this one…well, I doubted it would ever vanish.

It cut straight across my stomach, from left to right, without jagged edges. Whatever the creature used to slice people into corpses had hit me straight on. I was still alive thanks to my shadows, and the fact that it hadn't seen me.

Otherwise, I had no doubt that I'd be dead.

I took a deep breath of humid air as I combed my hair, looking into the steamed-up mirror. I had almost died. If the others hadn't found me quickly, if they hadn't been able to heal me, I *would* be dead.

I ran my finger across the scar, staring at it in the mirror, haunted by one question: who would mourn me when I was gone?

DRESSED AND PRESENTABLE, I stepped out of the bathroom. Glitter was exactly where I'd told him to stay, and it didn't look like he'd moved an inch. His eyes shifted slightly, to try to look at me. But he didn't turn his neck.

Okay. Maybe he was a bit too literal?

"You can move, now," I said. His shoulders relaxed and he seemed relieved. He turned his neck to look at me but didn't say anything.

"Okay," I asked, sitting down on my desk chair. "Why are you really in my room?"

"I told you," he started, but I held up my hand.

"The truth," I said softly. "It's okay, I won't be mad."

I braced myself, to make sure I could keep that

promise. Breathe in, breathe out, find all the limited patience in your heart…

"This place is safe," he said, the strange broken quality of his voice almost muted by its softness.

"The Guild of Shadows is a safe place," I agreed. "You don't need to be afraid here."

"No," he shook his head. "This place," he motioned to the room. Then he stopped and pointed at me. "You're safe."

"Oh. You wanted to stay with me?"

He nodded enthusiastically, hood bopping up and down.

"Dessert keep Glitter safe."

"My name is Tira," I mumbled. "And you're safe here, at the Guild of Shadows. You don't need to be *beside* me."

He blinked a couple of times, as though to ward away the confusion.

"No, you're the one who kept me safe. You save Glitter."

I sighed. He was twenty, like me. Like all of the Traded.

But Glitter seemed a lot younger. Or maybe he didn't have the same neurological or emotional scope that most Traded and humans did. He likely wasn't the only one. I'd heard rumors over the years of really different Traded. Like the one that looked like a rock and just sneezed once in a while. Or the one that looked like cheese. Rumor was that he'd been served as fondue in some billionaire's house. But I doubted that was true. I damn hoped it wasn't, anyway.

Glitter, however, could speak. He'd been selected for a researchers' guild, so he was smart. But maybe he didn't have the same filters or emotional bandwidth.

"You're scared," I said, looking at him with sympathy.

"No," he sounded sullen. "I just like being safe."

"Sounds like you're scared to me," I repeated, and he frowned, lowering his head beside the bed.

I guess I'd pissed him off. In retrospect, I could see why. He hadn't wanted to be called out on it. Maybe Glitter wasn't the only one who lacked a full emotional spectrum.

He shuffled and I leaned over to see what he was up to. He was squeezing under my bed. Is this what having a little brother felt like? I made a mental note to check under there for errant Traded before going to bed tonight.

My mind spun around for ideas on how to talk him out of there, but came up empty. A knock at the door thankfully distracted me.

I stood up and opened it.

"Can I come in?" Rachel asked as she pushed her way in.

"Sure, why not."

Rachel sat down on the edge of the bed. I opened

my mouth to tell her about Glitter, but didn't bother. I wasn't sure how to explain him, and it's not like I'd invited her to sit down anyway.

Served her right if she got spooked by a glowing-eyed mummy.

"I need to know what the creature looked like," Rachel said, her voice harsh, free of the singsong of the sea. Which wasn't unusual. She was more about the thunder and lightning than the waves, that one.

"I didn't even really see it," I said, sitting back down in my chair. I hated how tired I already felt, just from showering. Maybe I could beg off speaking to the guild leaders.

No. Then I wouldn't get to see Clay. I missed him so badly. I could do this for the chance to see him, even if just for a bit.

Clay would mourn me.

"But you *did* see it," she pushed. She apparently wasn't great at reading a room.

"As it sliced me, so I was distracted."

"It reacted with your shadows," she said. Okay, she'd been informed. Maybe everyone had been briefed. Which would make sense, I guess.

"It did," I agreed. She looked at me with fierce intensity, her eyes glued to me, leaning forward on my bed, arms stretched beside her as though any second, she would leap off and force details out of me.

I sighed. Might as well practice for the guild report.

"It shimmered when it struck my shadows, but I couldn't see it beforehand," I closed my eyes, tried to recall what little I had seen. "A blade cut me, but it seemed an extension of an arm, like the limb itself had been sharpened."

I frowned, trying not to linger in the moment it cut deeply, the pain exploding to the end of my extremities, as I struggled to hold my shadows near me. The shadows that had failed to shield me.

I found some comfort in the darkness behind my eyelids, though the light still pierced through. The light always pierced through.

Just like the creature's blade.

"The light," I said, opening my eyes and staring into Rachel's intent ones. "I think it was refracting the light to create some kind of cloaking system. That's why my shadows revealed it—not enough light could reach it.

Rachel's eyes seemed faraway for a few moments, like I'd told her that her favorite puppy had been pancaked. She stood stiffly.

"Thanks," she said. Before I could ask for more elaboration, she walked out of my room.

"You're welcome," I said to the closed door. I wanted little more than to crawl in bed for a rest, but I'd already slept too much, and Ian expected me to show up soon.

I heard slight shuffling under the bed. Yeah, that didn't make me want to crawl in bed, either.

"It's nothing to be ashamed or embarrassed of," I said to the otherwise empty room. "Fear, I mean. I hide in my shadows because they keep me safe," I debated not saying the next part, but my heart wasn't in denying Glitter what he needed from me. "If I make you feel safe, you can hang out with me."

A hesitant shuffle. The top of his head poked out from under the bed, his glowing eyes analyzing me.

"But you have to at least sleep in your own room."

He seemed about to protest, but then nodded and pulled himself out from under the bed.

"Okay," he said, taking an awkward step toward me. "Thank you," he patted my upper arm.

Then he shuffled back to the side of the bed and vanished.

"Are *you* scared?" he asked, a muffled voice behind the bed.

"I'm scared of speaking in front of the guild leaders," I admitted.

His head popped up beside the bed again. He stared at me for a moment.

"I'll come with you and make you feel safe," he offered.

I smiled. I couldn't imagine trying to explain Glitter to Clay. But I was glad I'd get the chance to try.

"Thank you," I said. "I think you'll like my friend Clay."

"I like friends," he agreed. "I didn't know you could have friends outside of your own guild."

"Well, we were friends at our academy beforehand," I smiled. This felt like an actual conversation with Glitter.

"So, you're no longer friends?"

"No, we still are. We're just not living together anymore, if that makes sense?"

"Yes," he nodded vigorously. Then he frowned, and started shaking his head. "No. All of my friends had to be from the Galileo Guild."

"I'm sorry," I said softly. "All of your friends are gone."

"Don't be sad," he said, half standing up. "They're not gone!"

"Your entire guild was killed."

"I didn't have any friends until I met you," he said. "And, since I don't have a guild anymore, I guess it's okay to be friends with someone from another guild."

"Oh." I guess I had a new friend.

"I won't get to be your friend when I go to another researcher's guild." He looked sad.

"No, we can still be friends!" I protested, not sure why I was protesting that. I mean, really, I'd be okay with not seeing him again, but he looked so sad, and he wasn't that bad…

Shit. How come I didn't mind stabbing people, and

yet I couldn't stand making the saddest person I'd ever met even more sad?

"How did you and Clay get to stay friends?" he asked, looking a bit happier.

"There are tests, as always," Glitter looked distressed. "Oh no, some are fun and easy!" I offered. "We had to recover a weird canister from another guild. I think they were a fighting league? I'm not sure. Anyway, then we had to bring it to the Wolf Pack League that Clay joined!"

"But you didn't pass the test," he said, looking even more distressed. "You were torn apart!"

"No, we weren't," I tried to sound firm. "We each had to go to our own guilds, but we can still chat."

Once every few months.

"You look sad," Glitter said, and I realized he was right beside me. I jumped.

"Back away, please," I said as calmly as I could. "Personal space, Glitter. Please stay an arm's length at all times, unless invited to come closer."

He nodded and took a step back. Exactly an arm's length away. Friendship with him wouldn't be too bad as long as I stayed patient and detailed my expectations.

Before I had to explain to Glitter that I wasn't sad—and before having to convince myself of that—a second knock came at the door.

It was time to face the leaders of the guilds.

12

Ian stared quizzically at Glitter.

"He's the only survivor of the Galileo Guild," I said. "He might have valuable intel." Glitter grinned at Ian.

"Do you?" Ian asked, arching an eyebrow and crossing his arms.

Glitter nodded and then stopped suddenly. "I don't think so. Maybe? It was all so fast…"

I folded my arms and looked at Ian. He sighed.

"I know that look. Fine, he can come, but only because he's the only one who can represent his guild anyway, and every guild was invited."

"Every guild?" I was surprised to hear that. "Isn't that a lot?"

"Maybe," Ian offered. "Look, we don't actually know how many guilds there are. But we know of some local chapters. We were invited by another research guild, and the Wolf Pack League offered their place as a secure neutral meeting ground. I'm not privy to the information of how many are coming."

"Aren't you worried?" I asked as we began walking toward one of the many side entrances. Rachel stood by her room, practically glaring at us. She looked like she wanted to come, but Ian gave no sign that she was invited. I wondered what her stake in this was. Maybe she was just aching for a good fight. To blow up the right people.

If I could create explosions, I'd probably want to go take out a few people, too.

"I'm always a little bit worried about everything," Ian offered once we were out of earshot of the trainees. "It's not a bad thing. It's kept me alive this long."

"Cheerful," I muttered. Glitter walked silently behind us, looking around him like he'd never seen anything quite like the Guild of Shadows. And, from his guild filled with books and decorative wood accents, he probably hadn't.

The walls were metallic, the bright light stole shadows (despite our name, which I thought was silly), and there were no enhancements or furnishings. Not even the leader's throne room proved to be spectacular. It wasn't his "throne room," I'd been informed early on. But it had a giant chair, so close enough as far as I was concerned.

Of course, these weren't our usual headquarters, I

was also told. Ian stayed here with us, but Sonsil ruled from the main Guild of Shadows outpost. They'd moved into this one to be closer to the canister and find it. It had been that important, and I still knew so little about it, except that it was part of a greater machine to open portals back up.

To bring us home.

It seemed impossible. But, at least, it meant that the fighter's league, where I'd stolen the canister back from, was just a ten-minute walk away.

Which proved rather convenient.

We stepped out of the southern side door, into the well-guarded alley. The first time we'd come here, we'd snuck in via this door. Some kind of shadow snare had blanketed it, and I'd never found out who had set it.

A mystery for another day.

So many mysteries, really, but it wasn't so bad. I'd see Clay soon, and we'd get to catch up, face-to-face. I was both elated and worried.

Three months ago, I'd stolen the canister from his league, after knocking him out. He knew it was me. And we hadn't had a good chance to chat since then.

Part of me worried about a blowout. But Clay was my oldest friend. I had to trust that he'd understand why I'd done it. To keep us both safe.

Apart, but safe.

I suddenly realized that we hadn't stopped by the armory.

"Weapons?" I asked, hopeful. Maybe he'd grabbed some for me already?

"No weapons," he answered. His glance flicked to my barrette, currently affixed to my belt, which hid a sleeping agent. It wasn't much of a weapon, but it would do in a pinch.

I guess the Wolf Pack didn't want a bunch of heavily armed Traded to invade its territory. I could understand that.

"Keep us in your shadows," Ian said. "It's probably a better way to go than via vehicle."

I nodded. Three people in my shadows should be doable.

I pulled every shadow, plentiful as the night had descended, around us. Every crack and corner offered a little bit of themselves, gathering around the three of us. I turned to Glitter, whose eyes were big and even more shiny. "Stay close," I whispered, "and don't talk."

He nodded and shuffled closer, then stopped, holding up his arm.

*What...*oh. Arm's length. I grabbed his arm and pulled him closer. Arm's length was a bit too far. Glitter looked confused but stayed the distance I placed him.

Ian stood as close as Glitter, but his presence wasn't uncomfortable. Not to me, anyway. Maybe because he'd been a puppy when we'd met, or maybe because he was a friend.

I glanced at Glitter, sticking close to me on my right, head bowed down, back hunched. Bandages covered what little I could see of his hands and face, robes hid his legs, a sweater provided a hoodie which hid his head and slightly droopy ears. I didn't want harm to come to him, either, even if he was weird. He depended on me in much the same way a puppy would.

Maybe I just liked dogs more than people? I really had to find out if the Guild of Shadows would let me adopt one.

We walked together, at a good clip, toward the Wolf Pack League. I focused so hard on keeping us safe that I hardly spared a thought to the anticipation of soon seeing Clay.

13

It AMUSED me that a tall building that looked like a really boring office tower housed one of the most popular fighting leagues. I dropped my shadows before we walked in, unchallenged. The doors were guarded. Unlike usual.

For a few moments, I allowed myself to imagine what the future would have looked like, had I joined them. Being here, in the arena, with Clay, instead of hiding in the shadows with my guild.

I liked the idea of fighting, but I didn't like their combats to the death. And I would never be able to fight Clay. Plus, the fighters' leagues were, at their heart, entertainment leagues. People watched them. Placed bets. Paid to see Traded tear each other to pieces...*no*.

This place wasn't for me. Not that the Guild of

Shadows would have allowed me to join it, but still. And, as much as I'd hated to admit it, this place worked really well for Clay.

"Tira!" I heard the familiar voice call as soon we went up a half-flight of stairs, leading to the "reception" area.

He half went in for a hug, but then changed to a fist bump, and the whole thing was just awkward as hell, but we both laughed and eventually hugged. He was all edges and muscle, his long hair tied back in a ponytail, his grin still as ridiculously easy as usual.

If you didn't know he was Traded and didn't look too closely, Clay could fool you into thinking he was human. But his teeth were a bit too sharp, as were his nails, forming claws. And, in the ring, he was fast. I'd seen a few of his combats, and his stats showed he had rarely been defeated. He'd reached Level 1 Champion status, which worried me.

To reach a higher level, he'd have to go for more dangerous fights. The type that could get you killed.

This place certainly bore little resemblance to the Guild of Shadows. The fighters were allowed to roam freely. Mind you, it also looked like an office decorated in the mid-80s, which wasn't great. Everything was kind of yellow gray and smoky looking.

Their arena, on the other hand, was high-tech fancy. And that was pretty much all I'd seen of the Wolf

Pack League. Except for the basement and cells, of course. I was good at getting thrown in those.

"What are you doing here?" Clay asked. "And what's that?" he pointed to Glitter, who still stuck very close to me. I hadn't even noticed he'd joined us.

"I'm Glitter," he said in his raspy voice, holding out his hand tentatively, not extending his arm all the way out.

"Clay," Clay said, grabbing the hand gently and awkwardly. I'd have laughed if it wasn't so sweet, in a weird way. Clay wasn't the gentle type, but he was trying, probably out of fear of breaking Glitter.

"Glitter is from the Galileo Guild," I said. Clay's eyes widened and he looked back at Glitter, as though really seeing him for the first time.

"You survived that attack?" Clay asked, sounding impressed and not a little bit skeptical.

"Dessert saved me! I mean, Tira!" Glitter grinned at me, looking pleased. I groaned. I'd forgotten to tell him not to mention that to Clay. I mean, I intended to tell him, eventually (probably), but not like this.

Clay's eyes targeted me and widened. "You were there?" The calmness of his voice didn't fool me. I knew he was upset. Maybe hurt.

"She saved me! Even saw the monster before it almost tore her in two!" Glitter added gleefully.

Wonderful.

Clay's eyes widened even more. Before I could shut Glitter up and tell Clay what happened, Ian joined us.

"The meeting is starting soon," Ian said, nodding to Clay.

"You almost got her killed," Clay spat, taking a step toward him. Ian stood taller than Clay, but Clay was all muscle. Ian didn't back down, holding his ground.

"Stop," I told Clay, my voice soft. "Please stop. Not here. Not now," I stepped between him and Ian, and glanced back further into the office space, where every fighter now glanced our way. I flushed bright purple.

I'd never get through this meeting.

Clay visibly struggled to get himself back under control, understanding that I didn't want to draw any more attention our way.

"We'll talk later," he told Ian, poison dripping from his words.

"If we must," Ian replied calmly. I thought Clay would just casually push me aside and smack Ian, but instead he turned around and led us into his league, toward the Boss' room.

I knew that place well.

It's where I'd stolen the canister, and where I'd betrayed Clay, choosing the Guild of Shadows over him. All this time, I'd been worried that Clay would be angry at me. But now I realized that he blamed my actions on Ian.

Ian didn't seem to care, but I did. Clay should know

that I could make my own choices, even if they weren't the ones he'd necessarily make.

We stepped into the Boss' room, her dark, piercing eyes staring at me from her bony face, shrewd and judging.

Sonsil stood near the Boss, speaking to another Traded, all green and mean-looking. This place was packed with serious-looking humans and Traded, guild leaders from near and far.

There were at least thirty. And I had to speak in front of all of them.

Tables formed a horseshoe, like a little United Nations. The overhead lights were so bright, they might as well be spotlights.

And it was expected that I would just stand there and reveal all of the details of my near death.

Shit.

Like I wanted to live through that again. In front of all these people. I tugged at the shadows around me, then let them float away. Ian had made me promise not to do anything to compromise the Guild of Shadows.

I regretted that promise.

"I can't do this," I mumbled, my hand automatically grabbing Clay's arm. Clay looked at me with some alarm.

"Can't do what? Are you okay?"

"She's fine," Ian stepped up. "Come on, Tira," he said

not unkindly. But Clay took another step toward him, as though he intended to protect me.

I sighed. I just wanted to be able to say when I didn't feel right, without having everyone turn it into a bar brawl. Before I could tell them both off (aka swear a lot), a shrill sound pierced the still air, then stopped.

Everyone froze and looked up

Someone had broken into the league. Where all of the guild leaders were gathered, ripe for the picking.

Oh good.

I felt strangely relieved. Facing the creature again proved a lot more alluring than facing the spotlight.

14

FOR A SPLIT SECOND, we stood frozen like a colorful tableau. Then all hell broke loose. The fighters stepped forward and began ushering their guests to various areas, I suppose splitting us up in the hopes the creature would be confused.

Ian marched toward Sonsil, sticking close to him as they shepherded him to the left. Sonsil looked annoyed. Ian glanced back to take stock of where I was.

"Tira!" He shouted and indicated I should follow. I started making my way through the throngs to reach him, but a hand clamped around my arm.

"Let's move," Clay pulled me in the opposite direction as Ian. I grabbed Glitter's sweater and dragged him along. He seemed confused and hunched further into himself.

I caught Ian's eye for a split second, and he looked

pissed, but stuck with Sonsil. If we all survived, I doubted I could stop Clay and him having that blowout.

I focused on the one inoffensive (if weird) participant here, Glitter.

"Stick with us," I told him. "Don't lose us." He looked up, shining green eyes wide with concern. "Clay'll take care of us," I grinned at him, then turned back, grip still firm on Glitter's sweater.

Clay dragged me to an office area, but not the one near the reception. A few offices lined the walls, surrounding several open-air desks in the central area. There were two entry points: the stairs, and the room we'd just arrived from. A few fighters ran by towards the stairs, wielding various and sundry weapons, to fortify the main entrance. Not that the creature generally took the main entrance as far as I could tell, but I could understand the impulse.

Clay dragged me and Glitter like extra baggage, into one of the offices. He opened a cabinet and pushed aside some old jackets, revealing a hidden door.

That was cool. I loved hidden doors. How many lurked in the Guild of Shadows? I'd have to double my efforts at finding them!

"This leads to the fire escape," he said. "You can escape from there."

He turned to go, and my heart dropped. I grabbed his arm.

"Like hell I'm leaving without you," I spat out, practically shaking. I held Glitter's sweater with my right hand still, and now held Clay with my left. Clay turned to argue with me, dark eyes intense, but I met and matched his glare.

Hell, I *doubled* it.

"We're *all* leaving *together*," I said. "Besides, Glitter and I are the only two who survived encounters with this thing," I shrugged, "so it makes more sense for the two of us to stay and you to go."

"Um," Glitter said behind me. "I have another idea."

"You do?" I turned to him, still hanging on to Clay but letting go of Glitter. Clay practically vibrated beside me. He didn't like being questioned, and he certainly didn't like that I was right.

"I can't believe that damn mutt put you in that creature's path," Clay muttered. I ignored him.

"I think I know what the creature wants," he said. "I've been studying it, you see." He grinned widely. He really did have nice teeth.

"What do they want?" Clay said, cracking his knuckles and shifting from foot to foot, hankering for a fight. I glanced at him, and we shared a grin. I didn't want to get cut again, but damn it would be good to fight together. Clay and I could handle anything together.

Always had. Always would.

I squeezed his arm and let him go as I summoned

my shadows and folded them gently and carefully to conceal the three of us. Glitter looked around with his strange eyes. I wondered what he saw through them. Maybe he could see my shadows in a way I wasn't able to?

I'd have to ask him. At a more opportune time.

"They want something that's supposed to open a portal," Glitter said, breathless, arms as extended as they could be, as though he spoke of wonder. Then his arms folded back in, the wonder leaking out of him. "But, I don't know what that is."

Clay and I shared a look. We knew exactly what it was. We'd been tested shortly after leaving the Margrave Academy with the retrieval of this item. And we'd almost paid with our lives.

Maybe we'd also paid a bit with our friendship.

I was the first to break eye contact, fearing that my cheeks were turning a bit too purple at the memory. I'd done what I'd had to do, for both Clay and me.

Still.

"Why do you think they're after something like that?" Clay asked.

Glitter glanced at me, then looked at Clay, all muscles and scowls right now. A shout was cut off, not far from us.

"It doesn't matter what they're after," I whispered. "We have to stay quiet." My shadows wouldn't exactly keep us hidden if we kept chatting among ourselves.

"And let my league get killed?" Clay practically spat out. "I'm going out there to help. Now that we know what they're after, we can maybe stop them…"

He stopped, avoided looking at me. Oh, he could stop them now, sure. By telling them it was at the Guild of Shadows and no longer here. By throwing my league under the bus, instead.

Damn proverbial bus.

"If we give it what it wants, it'll leave us alone?" Glitter half-asked, half-stated. He looked hopefully from Clay to me.

"Ya, I imagine it would," Clay said. Did I imagine the accusation in his voice?

"Fine," I said, grabbing two hangers from the closet. Sturdy wood with a metal hook. I tested them, one per hand, holding the base against my arm to steady it for hitting and blocking action.

I could work these. Hopefully they'd manage to do some damage.

"We'll go help. But stay within my damn shadows." I turned to Glitter. "You can stay here."

"Um," he looked at Clay, opened his mouth once before closing it, then reopened it. "I stay with dessert," he said resolutely.

"How do we even stop the damn thing," I mumbled. "It sliced me without even seeing me last time, Clay."

Half the people here are probably already dead, I wisely didn't say. Clay's hands gathered into fists. He wanted to help his league friends, of course. But I was the one he'd pulled to safety, I hoped not just out of habit.

"We make it show itself," Glitter said, the raspy voice somehow worse as a whisper. Quiet reigned in the rest of the building. I hated this quiet.

"And how do we do that?" I whispered, punching the air with my hangers. Clay handed me a dagger. It was well-weighted for throwing. I took it, but really wanted to try the hangers, first.

"We make it walk through something to make it create tracks, or to cover it all," Glitter said, looking pleased.

"Shit, that's stupid obvious," Clay mumbled.

"I'm embarrassed I didn't think of it either."

"Glitter is researcher," Glitter said, looking even more pleased.

"And a good planner," Clay amicably hit his shoulder. Glitter fell back, and I held him up. "Okay," Clay sounded excited. "We have a few things we can use. Paints, chalk, stuff like that."

"But where do we put it?" I asked. "Where even is it?"

"It'll go for the leaders, if it hasn't found them already," Clay said darkly.

"It'll go for the portal thing," Glitter offered.

Clay looked at me, and I shifted uncomfortably. "Well, Tira's the one it'll have to talk to, then."

"Clay, look…" before I could finish my sentence, the edge of my shadows shimmered.

My eyes widened and Clay followed my gaze, striking out with his axe as I threw my dagger. A double shriek pierced the air as we ducked, dragging Glitter down with us as blades cut the air above us.

"Move," I hissed. "Quietly!" The door was still closed. How the hell had it entered?

Clay flung it open and we threw ourselves out in a tumble.

But the creature wasn't far behind, and I'd dropped my shadows in the commotion.

We were sitting ducks.

15

CLAY TUMBLED TO THE RIGHT, away from me. Glitter held his head in his hands, looking for cover under a desk. I crouched, folding the shadows deep around me.

But that left Clay and Glitter without protection, and that thing could be anywhere with its deadly blades. I imagined one of them getting cut in two, not even having the chance to yelp...

No.

I pushed the shadows away from me, forcing them to form before me, to wrap themselves like a great shield around the opened door. Fueled by my adrenaline and fear, the shadows did as I bid. They formed like great wings, visible only to me and Glitter, whose eyes widened as he shuffled further under a desk.

I tightened my grip on the hangers and stood with

my feet apart, ready to move in any direction. Half a heartbeat passed (though it felt like a lifetime), before the creature stepped through my shadow shield. The shadows coated the creature, like a thick film, like chocolate in a mold, wrapping around it gently without hurting it, only revealing its shape without betraying anything else.

Like a ghost from my most terrible nightmares.

It wasn't that big—maybe five feet in height. With two sturdy legs, practically barrels, its shape seemed humanoid, with all the pieces where they should be. Except, instead of arms, it had four swords, one in each quadrant, sticking out. And its head was misshapen, like a triangle that turned into a rectangle halfway through.

My shadows revealed its shape and movement, but none of its finer details. It paused, its head shifting from side to side as though realizing its invisibility was compromised.

Now or never.

Before it could recover, I threw a hanger its way and managed to hit it in the head, where I hoped an eye might be.

But it didn't connect, going straight through it and bouncing off something in the office beyond it.

In those two eternal seconds, Clay had pushed himself back to his feet, pulled out a curved blade, and headed for the creature, bellowing a scream.

The creature ignored him, walking straight for me, sword arms extended.

"Shit," I threw myself back, keeping my shadows around it so that Clay would have something to target. Clay jumped from behind and landed a blow. This time, it connected, but the creature shrugged him off and sent him flying with a grunt, landing hard against a wall. Drywall and bricks shattered and tumbled on him, daylight breaking through the new hole.

Clay crumpled and didn't get up.

"Clay!" I shouted but turned back to the creature as it accelerated toward me, my shadows now revealing a glint of its eyes.

Intelligent, ferocious. Deadly.

And targeting me.

I kicked a chair its way and jumped over a desk, feet over my head, landing on the other side as gracefully as I could. It crossed the desk like it wasn't even there.

This was a hell of a lot more than just the ability to stay invisible. The desk hadn't shifted under it, or moved, or shimmered.

I took another step back, my last remaining hanger before me.

Shit. This wasn't going well.

I pushed my shadows against it, heart hammering in my ears, willing them to hold the creature steady.

For a split second, the creature paused and looked down in confusion. It studied my shadows, which tightened their grip, revealing more of the creature's details.

A chill ran down my spine. Not a creature. A man. No. A woman. A strong, angry, sword-bearing woman, with thick curls tight against her head, smart eyes narrowing as she approached.

Oh shit.

There was nowhere to go.

I shifted left, recalled my shadows to fold around me and quickly swerved right the moment I'd vanished.

The ruse would have worked, had her swords not been so damn long and struck my arm. I bit back a yelp, but she'd felt the contact and turned my way, four swords spinning around her chest like a circular saw.

I ducked, but she was wise to me, leaning down, invading my shadows, the twirling stopping as two of the swords united to created one long, sword-wielding arm.

She was deadly, but also kind of cool.

Being eviscerated by someone cool was better that by someone not cool, I guess?

I scrambled up, her sword coming down on me as I braced to at least try to block with my hanger…but the blow never connected.

The sword stopped in midair. Glitter had stepped in front of me, standing much straighter than before. He held his hand up before the woman, his fingers spread out, elbow bent.

For a split second, the creature didn't move. Neither did Glitter. And neither did I, hanger still before me, crossed arms protecting my head. The stale air turned sweet.

Then the warrior-woman-creature-thing moved, vanishing out of my shadows.

"Where did she go?" I asked, coming around to face Glitter. For a second, I didn't see the goofy grin and green, unblinking eyes. A mask of seriousness hid his mummified features.

"Glitter?" I asked. He blinked, and then the goofy smile re-appeared on his face.

"Did I do it?" he said, his voice raspy.

"I don't know what you tried to do, but where did she go?"

I gripped my hanger like my life depended on it.

"She's gone!" Glitter said. "I made her want sushi."

"I'm sorry?" I squinted around me, rippling my shadows out to see if I could reveal her. The shadows followed the waves of my adrenaline.

"I can plant suggestions," he said, still grinning. "And make people want things."

"Oh," I paused. "Wait. Did you do that to me?"

"No," he looked stricken. "Not to friend."

Clay!

I'd forgotten all about him, with my worries of

being cut in two. I ran to him and pulled him from the rubble. He was knocked out, sporting a bad cut across his arm, but he was alive. I swallowed hard, gently wiped some dust from his face.

Too close.

"You sure she's gone?" I whispered to Glitter.

"Sushi is very good," he offered. He glanced down at Clay's arm. "Bandage?"

I looked at him and the dirty bandages wrapping his body skeptically. He pulled out some fresh bandages from his hoodie's pocket.

"Thanks," I said, and quickly wrapped up Clay's arm. It would need redressing soon, but at least this staunched the flow.

"Okay," I told Glitter. "Stay here with Clay. I'll find help."

I handed him my hanger.

"Um, okay," he said, holding it gingerly with two fingers as though it was covered in spiders.

"In case she comes back."

"Is there sushi near?"

"No. In case she breaks free of your suggestion."

"Okay," he said. "I won't see her without your shadows."

"Just...stay here. Be quiet. Lay low. Keep Clay safe."

He looked even more incredulous as I spoke. I sighed. "I promise I won't be long."

"Okay," he said, and I turned to head back toward the Boss' chamber. I glanced back at Glitter and Clay.

Damn it, Clay. If you don't get better before we've had a chance to clear the air, I'll never forgive you.

Or myself.

16

I STEPPED into the chamber which Clay had dragged me out of earlier. Apparently, he'd dragged me out just in time. Bodies covered on the floor. I recognized some of the fighters from his league. I hoped none were Clay's friends.

There were also bodies from the various leagues, guilds, organizations…all Traded who had gathered here.

Equally slaughtered, without rhyme or reason.

"Tira," I heard the gasp behind me. I turned, to see Clay there, Glitter by his side. Clay looked shaken, but at least he was standing. I clasped hands with him. He looked as happy to see me as I was to see him.

I felt relieved, adrenaline pumping out of my blood. But now wasn't the time for a heart-to-heart.

"I have to find Ian and Sonsil," I said, my own voice distant in my ears.

"This is my league," pain laced his voice, which was much worse than the anger I'd expected.

"Not all of the bodies are from your league," I said gently. "Where did the rest hide?" He looked up slowly at me, as though trying to focus on me. "Where did the rest of them go, Clay?"

"Down," he said, "the rest of my league was gonna take shelter downstairs," and he ducked out of the door. I bit my lower lip. Damn it. Ian and Sonsil had slipped out another door, but Clay was alone and they had each other at least...

"Damn it," I muttered and followed Clay, who'd already reached the stairs. Glitter stayed behind amidst the corpses, his green glowing eyes wide as he looked at the slaughter at his feet.

Clay practically jumped down three flights of stairs before I reached him. "Wait," I whispered urgently. "We don't know where the monster is."

"Sushi," Clay said. "Glitter said she went for sushi."

"Okay, but does he seem like the most stable and in-touch-with-reality person you've ever met?"

"Good point," Clay slowed down and stuck close so that I could wrap my shadows around us both. The shadows didn't fight me, welcoming my embrace. Their usefulness had morphed into something more.

Like an extension of me. I'd managed to use them in a completely different way.

It had been exhilarating. And terrifying.

And I hoped damn hard it was replicable.

We reached the basement and Clay grinned back my way, though I could see the worry in his eyes. I nodded to him and crossed the threshold, into the corridor.

I knew this place. I'd once come here to pick up Clay's body, after he'd been poisoned by Ian. It hadn't felt quite this ominous before, the flickering lights messing with my shadows. Keeping them steady with the fluctuating light proved tough, but my motivation was damn high.

Clay indicated with his head that we were heading left. If I recalled correctly, that room held the garbage receptacles.

The stench wafting from it confirmed my memory.

Great.

"We weren't sure it could navigate by scent," he whispered and shrugged. I stuck my tongue out in disgust.

Clay opened the door, the stench intensifying, my stomach jumping in my throat. Awesome. That's what this day needed.

I tried not to think of sushi.

Damn Glitter.

Clay breathed out, and I realized he'd been holding his breath, not because of the stench (which was why I held mine), but because of his worry. I dropped my shadows, and the other fighters and Wolf Pack members saw Clay, smiles lighting their faces. A line of armed fighters, ready to stand to protect the others, broke and met Clay, hugs and fist bumps shared all around.

They were safe. That was good. Clay was happy. That was also good.

I was still worried about Ian and Sonsil. That was less good.

I looked at Clay, among his own.

His own. How far we'd come. And he'd never forgiven me for betraying him and giving the canister to the Guild of Shadows. That had been made clear.

And, now that it had cost so many of his league's members' lives, he never would. I swallowed hard and turned around. I was almost out of the room before a hand caught mine.

"I'll come with you," Clay said, squeezing my hand gently. I smiled slowly at him.

"Thanks," I said.

"I've got your back," he answered, with barely any hesitation. "For old time's sake."

"Right."

He let go of my hand and we walked back up together.

17

ACTIVITY HAD RESUMED in the league, most of it rather morose. Bodies were being moved, mourned over. Adrenaline gave way to grief. A few injured received healing, but not many. Most who had encountered the intruder hadn't survived.

"They took her," one of the Traded reported to the Boss. "They took Lorna." I recognized the name, but only because Clay had told me who she was. A Traded who looked like an old woman.

I had limited sympathy for her. She'd messed with Clay's mind before, getting him to almost kill me. But she was also a Guild of Shadows operative, as far as I could tell. She could fold shadows too, in a different way than I could. I guess it hadn't saved her, in the end.

Where could she be? And why would they take her and not kill her? And when exactly had they done that?

All the edges of the Boss' face were hard as always, but something in her eyes softened for a split second. She turned and spotted me, her gaze settling on me.

"I'm sorry," I said, hoping she'd focus her attention elsewhere.

"She's been with me for years," she said to me, though I suspected she'd have spoken to a plant if that were closer. I just happened to be the nearest sentient thing. "I shall miss her loyalty."

I certainly wasn't about to tell her that I was pretty sure she was from the Guild of Shadows. "Has she been with you for the whole twenty years she's been on this planet?" I couldn't think of anything else to say.

She turned to look at me, as though seeing me for the first time. "Twenty years? Did she look twenty to you?"

I shrugged. "Well, no, but we all came over twenty years ago, so some of us must age at different speeds, I suppose."

"Oh, but you are a simple child, aren't you?" She walked away, not saying anything else to me.

Wow, thanks old woman.

"Tira," Ian seemed beyond relieved to see me. Glitter stuck close to him, though Ian ignored him. I smiled at both of them, genuinely glad to see them.

"Are you and Sonsil okay?" I asked, unable to spot the leader of the Guild of Shadows in the throngs of bodies.

"We are," he said, his voice turning to a growl. "Though many weren't so lucky."

I glanced at the ground slick with blood. My head pounded, nausea slithering inside me. Clay helped others move bodies, looking grim, his jaw clenched. His arm must be hurting like hell, but he didn't mention it, the quick patchwork job I'd done already bleeding through.

I wondered if Traded ever got vacation. I should ask. I could use one right about now. And so could Clay.

"You should have stayed," Ian said, so low I barely heard him.

"I'm sorry," I said, meeting his eyes. I'd rarely seen Ian pissed off. His dark eyes were narrow, his posture perfectly still, his nostrils slightly flared.

"You should have stayed with Sonsil and I. Guild members have to keep each other safe."

"Clay dragged me out," I said, knowing it sounded lame.

"If you can't break free from Clay's grasp, then you are definitely not ready for the field."

Ouch. That hurt on multiple levels. And I doubted he meant physically breaking free, too.

"You're right," I said gently, looking toward Clay. "Some things are hard to break free of."

"Especially when you don't want to," Ian whispered, the anger dissipating from him.

"Ian," I started to say, but was interrupted.

"Ms. Misu," a tall fighter walked up to me. Ian stepped in front of me, Glitter behind me. I sighed, and gently placed my hand on Ian's shoulder to push him aside. He relented a bit, but stayed slightly in front of me regardless.

A second fighter joined the first. A shock of blue hair stuck up at the top of his head. I'd fought this one before. He was good. But I'd gotten better since last we'd fought. A rematch might prove interesting.

"The leaders would like a word with you," the taller of the two fighters said. I spotted a name badge embroidered on his brown jacket. Oh. That was useful.

"The leaders, Jon?" I said. "I'm sorry?"

He didn't seem bothered by me knowing his name. I was reviewing my conception of the fighter's league as just barbaric. I mean, name badges were just nice ice breakers.

Plus, I respected the name Jon without an "h."

"Including the Guild of Shadows," he said, nodding to Ian.

"Okay," I said, "Jon without an h. I'm sorry, am I saying your name right?"

"It's said the same, yes."

"It's just you're missing an h, and I want to make sure I'm not being unnecessarily insulting. I do like the name badges."

"Ms. Misu," Jon said, sounding exasperated. I

glanced at the second blue-haired warrior. He didn't have a name badge.

"You're just not friendly ever, are you?"

He shrugged, but I could see his grin through the fabric of his mask.

"Last time, you almost killed him," I said, indicating Ian with my head.

"I didn't realize who you were," he said, apologetically. "Obviously."

"Obviously," Ian agreed, though his voice was anything but friendly. "Why do they want to see Tira? And you say Sonsil is among them?"

"Yes," Jon said. "We're reviewing the footage of the attack to understand the creature. We saw some interesting battle techniques on the part of Ms. Misu."

Ian raised an eyebrow but didn't fully turn to look at me.

"We go because Sonsil asks, for no one else," Ian said softly. "Is that clear?" He glared at the warrior, who met his eyes but seemed uncomfortable.

Clay joined us, glaring at Ian. Ian didn't even bother glaring back, which made me feel worse. Had he given up on me? On me ever being able to break free from Clay to become a full-fledged operative of the Guild of Shadows? What happened if I didn't? It's not like they could fire me and send me out into the streets, could they?

Glitter stepped beside me, taking hold of my arm to indicate that he didn't intend to be left behind.

"You'll be fine," Clay told me, his voice loud enough for Ian to hear. I doubted the words were for me. "The Wolf Pack isn't a bunch of killers like some other guilds, after all."

"Let's just get this over with," I said, annoyed at Clay. And Ian. And myself. I walked past Ian and Clay to follow the two fighters.

Glitter followed along quietly, and his glowing green eyes were the most comforting thing about this entire group.

18

We passed through several corridors and up another flight of stairs that I hadn't even known existed. Turned out what I'd seen of the league so far was just a front to a much bigger, more opulent side. Where sad offices lined the main floor, all full of dust and crappy carpeting, this part of the league had been recently renovated.

Floors and walls mimicked the look of ancient castle walls, great stones buttressing our walk. Light sconces lined the wall like torches, every third one a different colour, reflecting off the strange coating on the rocks to make it seem like we were under water.

Or at a rave?

I'd never been in either, so I wasn't sure. But it was definitely mind-bending.

It didn't feel like we were in an old shitty office

building anymore. The place felt rich, warm, and slightly psychedelic.

I loved it and turned to grin at Clay. He kept looking forward morosely. I turned with my grin to Ian. Same.

Glitter's eyes shifted as he examined his surroundings. I couldn't tell if it was with awe, but I was glad to see that at least one other person seemed to be impressed and not moping. The day had been terrible—might as well enjoy some nice sights.

We went up a carpeted (red!) stairway, into another, wider corridor. The adjoining rooms didn't have doors, but great stone archways instead. I glanced into the first to see racks brimming with weapons, like a great medieval armory.

"Shit, that's cool," I mumbled to no one in particular. Only Glitter nodded as he kept looking around.

The second room featured more modern weapons. Hell, very modern—some of them I didn't even recognize, including types of guns that I had no clue what they did.

But they looked cool! I badly wanted to head in there and maybe take a grenade or two. Glitter's idea about making the creature show itself had been solid, and I'd used my shadows to make it happen. But I had to compromise my own invisibility to do so, and if I could avoid that in the future...well, that would be more than okay.

Some of those grenades could be adapted or might already be adapted. Not every combat here was to the death, after all.

And Clay complained that my Guild was all murdery. At least we didn't kill each other for sport!

Our guards abruptly stopped in front of us.

"Don't draw weapons in the presence of the Boss," Jon said. "Those are the rules. If you do, you will be killed."

"Fine," I said, when Clay and Ian didn't answer. The hanger hung at my belt, but I somehow doubted those were the kinds of weapons they referred to. "But, just to be clear, is that the only scenario that will get us killed?"

"No," Jon walked forward.

My hand twitched to reach for my hanger and just leave, but Ian gently placed his hand on my wrist, without bothering to look over, as though reminding me to behave.

I sighed and nodded. His hand moved away.

Two large, thick wooden doors, engraved with guild symbols, opened dramatically before us. Guards from the Wolf Pack League stood beyond them.

The light changed in quality—now purple and shimmery. I recognized some of this. It looked a bit like the ripple of my shadows, though it did something with the light, instead.

I glanced down, then sideways, between the stones still lining the corridors around us, to the wall behind the guards…"they're hiding the shadows."

"Don't go invisible now, please," Ian said, almost at the same time as Clay said: "Don't vanish."

The two glared at each other, even though they'd both offered the exact same advice. I ignored them and analyzed the light further.

It seemed pretty ridiculous, hiding my shadows now. Unless they thought their defenses might also reveal the creature? But the creature used light to hide itself, as far as I could tell, like the refractions used for some camouflage gear.

I wished they'd turn this light off, whatever it was. Or at least have them explain it to me. I hated things that broke my shadows, but maybe if I understood them more, I could at least respect them.

We walked into the large room and I looked up in surprise. The ceiling tripled in height, leading to a large, finely decorated dome. Gold leaf trimmed stonework, intricate painted murals were book-ended by pastel lit glasswork, the entire ceiling a chandelier for the room.

All of it casting that strange light that ripped away the shadows.

The shadows that had just saved me. Hell, saved all

of us. Even though Glitter had managed to get the creature moving, it hardly meant that it wouldn't return. And, without my shadows to see it by, he might not have been able to stop it.

I wondered how powerful Glitter truly was, under his wrappings and glowing eyes.

"Tira Misu of the Guild of Shadows, please step forward," a voice boomed. I'd been so busy looking at the light and ceiling that I'd forgotten that people would be here.

Turned out that I much preferred shadow-stealing light to this many people.

The Boss, skin tightly wrapped around fine bone structure, white hair swept up, dark eyes permanently narrowed in disgust, sat in a large, gilded chair. Her dress seemed simple enough, but the drape of the fabric led me to think it was probably worth a gazillion dollars. Several rings, bracelets and necklaces picked up the purple of the light and shone perfectly.

I wondered if she selected her jewelry based on the light. That would be pretty smart.

Surrounding her were guild leaders, all standing. I spotted Sonsil, who looked more annoyed than I'd ever seen him. His dark skin and bald head seemed to shun the purple light, as though he had better things to do than be whimsical.

Which, as far as I could tell, was Sonsil's modus operandis.

He glanced my way and gave a slight nod, and then focused on Ian. I figured the two were having an entire conversation made entirely of minute facial movements, and I wasn't privy to any of it.

Clay squeezed my arm and stepped back. He dragged Glitter with him, though Glitter looked like he wanted to stay with me.

Ian, however, stayed by my side. He looked at me encouragingly, though I could see the grimness still clinging to his eyes. He took a step back, leaving me at the forefront. This was apparently Guild of Shadows spotlight time.

Which was ridiculous. What the hell didn't people get about the Guild of *Shadows*? Come on! It wasn't that hard!

I stopped a ways off from the Boss. I endeavored to ignore the assembled leaders and tried desperately to keep my tail from swishing from side-to-side.

I felt so very purple right now. My horns probably shone purple, even though they were usually black and could fit in with my hair. I wondered if they'd be more hidden if I did an updo like the Boss. Maybe she'd give me hair tips.

I looked at her perma-scowl.

Maybe not. Besides, she'd already insulted me once today. Probably best not to give her further ammunition.

"We've been reviewing footage of the attack," the

Boss said. She lifted her hand, and the footage began playing to her left. I couldn't even see the screen, like the projection happened midair.

I had definitely underestimated the technological coolness of the Wolf Pack League.

There was no sound, but I could see the creature and my shadows intermix. I cringed again at the sight of Clay collapsing. I spotted Glitter, crouched in a corner, as though he struggled between running away and standing up for his friends.

He decided just before I was about to get cut in two, apparently frozen in place.

Well, that was embarrassing. I hadn't been frozen, per se. Just out of ideas. Maybe I could offer that addendum.

The projection stopped, the strange purple lights flooding the room again. As a distraction, I tried pulling a few shadows, but the second I found them in the tiniest of cracks, they vanished in the weird light. I stopped seeking them out, feeling bad they kept flickering out of existence.

Ian placed his hand on my elbow, a tiniest brush, and I realized that no one was talking. I focused back on the people around me (so many people) and realized that they were all looking at me.

Too many people.

I struggled against calling the shadows to me, knowing it wouldn't work. My next instinct was to run, but Ian's hand on my elbow left me to believe that this gentle touch would turn to a vice grip if I even tried.

I could probably take Ian.

But then, he could turn into a bear and squeeze me.

Yeah, he'd win.

Shit.

Sweat dripped down my back. I'd been fine for the whole battle with the creature, but this was different. This was shittier, and I hated being the center of attention.

Hated it with an ever-growing passion.

"How did you do that, Ms. Misu," the Boss said, her voice crisp as always. I wondered if she always sounded like she was threatening someone. *Pass the salt, or die.*

"I used my shadows?" I offered. Ian's hand didn't change or shift in its pressure. Okay. I guess I was doing okay, or at least not completely terrible.

"You revealed the creature to us," the Boss said, and the leaders all moved with interest.

"I don't think we should call it a creature anymore," I said. Ian groaned softly beside me. "I mean, it's a Traded, right? And we know it's a woman, or I'm going to guess anyway, because she was so cool. So maybe we should give her a name. Like Annie?"

The Boss glared at me. My nerves churned my words to life.

"Okay, not Annie," I mumbled. "You pick."

"I don't care how we address this monster," the Boss said. I was pretty sure at least she was human, but not positive. She was definitely cranky, though. "How did you make it show itself?"

"If you turn off your weird lights, I'll show you," I offered.

"Our full-spectrum lights reveal the creature's blood," one of the guards said. "It's the only way we have of revealing its presence."

"Well, they didn't stop it from entering, did they?" I said, now annoyed. "So obviously it can do other stuff. And, besides, Glitter is the one who got the creature to back off of me, so you might want to talk to him?"

Glitter shrivelled beside Clay, and I felt bad for shifting the spotlight to him.

"We're aware of what the researcher can do," the Boss said.

"I filled in a form," Glitter offered.

"There's a form?" I shrugged. "Look, I can't show you if I can't draw the shadows."

The Boss's eyes caught mine, and she seemed to be weighing the fiber I was made of. She'd already seen me in her arena, against my will. She'd seen me grieve Clay, when I thought him dead. But she sought something else.

Would I betray her?

I held her gaze. No, I wouldn't betray her. Because

Clay's life was hers to do with as she wished. She seemed to make up her mind and nodded to the guard.

The quality of the light changed, becoming less purple, and less all-invasive. I didn't know which spectrums "full-spectrum lights" targeted, but they did seem fairly comprehensive.

I called the shadows to me. Ian tightened his grasp on my elbow.

Damn it, Ian. I just wanted to slip out. I folded the shadows around me and him, and turned to him, frowning.

He shook his head. We could still be heard, after all. I debated stabbing Ian with my barrette, releasing the sleeping agent in it into his blood stream, so he'd snooze off my escape.

But I suspected that Ian was immune to it. Plus, he could easily track me down.

I rolled my eyes at him and dropped my shadows.

The light changed again and became all-invasive.

"Can I go, now?" I said. I'd been so comfortable in my shadows, that now the light felt like it burned. Ian sucked in his breath.

Well, it's not like I could tell them more. And I certainly couldn't tell them what Glitter had told me, about being after the "portal material," aka the canister the Guild of Shadows had stolen from the Wolf Pack League. I didn't know if they suspected it had been us, but probably best not to shine a light on that particular detail.

The Boss flicked her wrist, indicating I was dismissed.

I glanced at Ian, and gave him a look that I hope meant "be careful" and not just "good luck, I'm getting the hell out." I quickly stepped outside, walking until the shadows grew plentiful and welcoming.

Clay and Glitter trailed me, but I didn't care.

Right now, I just wanted to be with my shadows. Hidden and safe.

"Tira," Clay said, catching up to me before I could vanish. Glitter stayed near, but a bit back, giving us at least a semblance of privacy.

"Thanks for patching me up," he said, holding up his arm, where the bandage was now crooked and covered in blood.

"Pretty sure I should do that again."

"That's okay," he said. "I can visit one of the healers."

"Oh. Of course." This wasn't like the old days. We didn't have to sneak around and not get caught. We weren't just two in the whole world, looking out for each other when everyone else wanted us dead... "This is weird," I said.

"Agreed. I mean, it's not bad though. Is it?" he looked sideways at me. I sighed and stopped, motioning for Glitter to stay a bit away. He folded in on himself but did as asked.

"Are we still friends?" my voice was calm, which surprised me. I thought my heart would tear in two just a few months ago when we had to join different guilds. Now? He was home. I had my own home. And we had healers and different friends.

Well, *he* did, at least.

"Of course we are!" he said. Then he took a deep breath. "Look, I'm still mad at you for taking the canister," he said, then looked up and down the corridor to make sure we were alone. Glitter mimicked his movement, then grinned and nodded to us, moving a tad closer. He'd be our lookout.

We knew they had cameras. But they didn't seem to have sound on them, or at least the playback earlier hadn't had any. It wouldn't hurt to be quieter. Clay lowered his voice.

"I'd never betray you, Tira. I didn't just now, did I? And I know you took the canister because you were forced to. That guild is no good, Tira."

"Clay, your guild is the one that made us steal it in the first place! How is it any different than the Guild of Shadows?"

"Because your guild did it to tear us apart!" Clay spat out. I took a step back, surprised by his intensity. He seemed just as surprised, but pushed on. This was different for Clay. He usually sulked and didn't share much. "That's the difference with your guild. You break stuff. You hurt others. You work in the background and no one really knows what you do!"

"That's not true and you know it! We're here, after all," I said, frowning. "We're hardly hiding."

Ian's words pounded the back of my head, giving me a headache. I couldn't be a full Guild of Shadows operative until I broke free of Clay's grasp. One betrayal wasn't enough.

What did they want from me? What did Clay want? Why couldn't people just leave me alone?

"You're here because the Boss knows you exist," Clay pushed on. "Because not to come would be an insult to the Pack. But, Tira, see what I mean? Don't you get what you did? What you're doing? That place will change you!"

"Oh, come off it, Clay," the whole argument sapped whatever energy I had left. "How have I changed? How? I still just want to hide in my shadows. I still follow you into ill-thought-out ideas. I still bandage your wounds."

My voice sounded tired in my own ears. I sighed. "Look. This is what it is. We can still be friends, though, but only if you're okay with it. You're the one who'll eventually get killed in the arena, and I'll probably have to watch it," I stopped, redirected, not able or willing to even imagine Clay's death. Not so soon after almost witnessing it. "It's not like we're given some nice, quiet retirement option, Clay. I just, I don't know, I just think this is what we've got, and we can make it work. Right?"

His jaw tightened. "What did you do with the canister, Tira?"

"Does it matter?"

"You were willing to trade our friendship for it."

"Of course not," those words hurt, probably because they partly rang true. "I did it to protect you, Clay. A lot of what I do is to protect you."

Clay considered for a few moments, his dark eyes searching mine, looking for the girl he grew up with, his best friend for years, the one who protected him and kept him safe, who fought by his side, who laughed the darkness away.

He gently placed his hands on my shoulders, came closer. I could feel his breath on my face, and my heart raced. I didn't even mind the purple flush of my cheeks.

"I still don't like it," he said. "But, yeah, we're still friends. Forever."

I saw him then. My Clay. All anger and vulnerability, all power and little direction, all fight and fire. He was scared. For me, for himself.

For us.

I reached for his neck, pulled him to me, and kissed his lips. Then pulled away.

"Damn right we are," I said, breathless.

We walked toward the entrance together, not needing to tell each other anything more. I felt more free than I had for months. Not since stealing the canister. Screw being an operative if it meant betraying where I came from. Clay was right about one thing: the Guild of Shadows wanted to change me. To drag me away from Clay.

But that didn't mean I had to accept it. Or go along with it.

For the first time in a long time, the silence between Clay and I felt comfortable, and I didn't sense the urge to fold my shadows.

It was nice that something good came out of all this shittiness.

19

By the time we got back to the Guild of Shadows, I was exhausted. Adrenaline and emotional rushes, plus having to speak in front of the assembled guild leaders, had all taken a toll. Okay, the speaking in front of people had by the far been the worse. After a silent walk, we entered the same entrance we'd exited.

I let my shadows relax, feeling their flexibility around me. I'd covered Sonsil, Ian, and Glitter on the way back. Four people when I could barely conceive of covering five just a couple of days ago.

If I could thank the creature-warrior-not-Annie for one thing, it was motivation to get better, faster.

Sonsil broke from our group as soon as we entered the safety of the Guild. Ian stopped and looked pointedly at Glitter.

"Go to your room and stay there until you're called,"

he told Glitter, leaving no room for discussion. Glitter hesitated before his shoulders dropped and he shuffled down the hall.

Ian indicated that I should follow him. I did, silently. Ian was still annoyed, which could be bad. A few weeks ago, I'd tried sneaking out (and failed miserably), and had been assigned to clean all the toilets in the Guild, plus six straight hours of training.

That had been a tad tiring.

He brought me to a door I'd never managed to open (not for lack of trying). The initiates were given access to their rooms, training areas, rec areas…but not any of the higher-level Guild areas. I suspected they had a better Mission Room there, too.

Ian placed his hand on the lighter metal area of the door, and it slid sideways. It must be linked to biometrics, making it hard to break into.

Hard, but not impossible.

The corridor beyond it looked disappointingly like every other corridor in the Guild. I was hoping for something more impressive. I mean, the Wolf Pack League had all this fancy stuff beyond the front-facing offices. Why couldn't we at least get a piece of art, instead of just metallic walls?

So. Much. Metal.

Maybe the actual headquarters of the Guild of Shadows, which I'd yet to see, would wow me. If I ever got to see them, anyway.

I followed Ian down two corridors. He kept his hands casually folded behind his back. I recognized it as his "don't you dare challenge me" look. Combined with his looking up and down the corridor regularly, I assumed he wasn't supposed to bring me here. Finally, we reached a door, which he opened using the same biometric pad.

He indicated with his chin that I should walk in. I did, a smile splitting my lips at the fresh scent, before I even saw the wonders within.

The room overflowed with plants, gentle lights shining over them, accentuating the various greens and the vibrant colors of countless flowers, and sparkling off the fountain gurgling in a corner. Rocks were generously strewn around, a trail leading to a cave partially hidden by strands of ivy.

It was like being outdoors, except indoors.

"Is this your room?" I asked in awe. This place screamed Ian and wildlife.

"It was a concession Sonsil was willing to make."

"I'm glad," I gently cupped a flower in my hand, its yellow petals bright against my skin. "This place is magic."

"Well," he sounded embarrassed. "I generally shift to sleep. If I can't, I wake up shifted anyway. So, this makes more sense."

"It makes you more comfortable," I said. He looked even more embarrassed. "No, that's good. It's like my shadows. They make me feel safer. Feeling safe is important, Ian."

He sighed. "It is. And feeling supported is important, as well."

I let go of the flower and turned to face him. "I'm sorry I made you feel unsupported," I sighed. "I just lose my head a bit with Clay, I guess." I remembered kissing him, and flushed. Damn it. Ian probably saw that.

"That's not it," he said, shaking his head slowly. "I mean, *I* didn't support *you*."

Now that, I hadn't expected. "You supported me," I said softly, remembering him staying with me when I had to stand before the Boss.

"No, you shouldn't have had to do any of that," he looked frustrated, but I didn't think it was with me. I waited for him to finish, even though I just wanted to comfort him. Ian was a good friend. I hated that he thought differently.

"I'm worried," he admitted, pacing up and down. I sat on a rock and listened. It seemed like that's what I'd been brought here to do.

"It's Sonsil," he said, forcing himself to stay still. He stood in front of me. "Something's going on, and I don't know what it is. It's worrying me."

"You think it has something to do with the canister?"

"Maybe. Yes." He spoke more softly, as though he

couldn't believe he uttered the words. "It does. I'm sure of it. And our involvement with it."

"And the attacks," I added, remembering Glitter's words.

Ian narrowed his eyes, and then sighed and sat down on a rock opposite me. "I shouldn't be surprised anymore when you know things you really shouldn't, but delight me with details—how exactly do you know that?"

"Glitter told me," I said. "He's been researching the warrior, and thought she was after something related to the portal."

Ian sat quietly for a few minutes. I knew he absorbed the information and distilled it, adding it to the information puzzle in his mind.

"How did he find that out?" he finally asked.

I shrugged. "He's a researcher." Ian raised an eyebrow slowly. "Okay, maybe we need to question Glitter. But nicely! Poor guy's been through a lot. We don't need to hurt him."

"No, I don't think we need to hurt him," Ian said. "Do you think we would?"

"If necessary? Yes."

He looked at me quietly, and I thought I saw sadness in his eyes. "You're right. Would you hurt him if it had a greater purpose, Tira?"

"Like maintaining the balance? Keeping the Traded and humans safe? Maintaining the peace?" I managed to keep the sarcasm out of my voice.

"Yes," he said softly.

"Ian, none of that exists now, so there's nothing to maintain. A Traded is slaughtering us. What even are we trying to maintain?"

"Survival," Ian whispered. He looked tired. I resisted the urge to walk up to him and gather him in my arms. "If we don't get this under control, Tira, it might get out of hand. The Traded will all be in danger from humans if it slips out. We're honestly lucky it's only picked on us so far."

"It doesn't feel lucky," I muttered, remembering the piles of bodies.

"It's better than it could be," his voice picked up strength again. "And I need you to believe that. Look, Tira, you're the only one who managed to reveal the creature. You survived an encounter with it. Twice!"

"So did Glitter," I offered.

"Because he was with you," Ian said. "How did you manage to get your shadows to do that, anyway?"

"I..." I paused, thought back to that moment. Clay and Glitter needed me. We were all going to die, unless I revealed our assailant. I looked up to Ian. "Survival."

"Survival," Ian nodded.

"You're not just worried about this thing killing us, are you?"

"No," he placed his elbows on his knees and his chin

in his hands, observing me closely. "Can I trust you to keep something a secret? Even from Clay?"

"I don't know that I'd get the chance to tell Clay anyway," I shrugged.

"Tira."

"I got the canister back for the Guild of Shadows, didn't I? My loyalties may seem split, but as long as I can keep Clay safe by falling in line, I will. Always."

"I know," Ian said. "And I am sorry about that. But they will use Clay against you time and time again to keep you in line."

I nodded, swallowing hard. I wondered if that was why Ian wanted me to break from Clay. Not because he didn't like Clay, though I knew he didn't, but because it was like a big control button on my life.

Ian wanted me to be as free as I could be. And to keep Clay safe by not having him as leverage.

"Thank you," I said.

He looked perplexed. "For what? We're friends, aren't we? Friends look out for each other."

Perhaps due to exhaustion, tears began to gather in my eyes. I simply nodded. Ian was a different friend than Clay, that's all. It didn't mean he was a bad friend. Just...different.

"Okay," he said, as though confident I wouldn't betray his thoughts. "I'm afraid these attacks have a secondary purpose of making Traded reveal their true potential."

"Isn't that what the schools were for? To test us?"

"Yes," Ian said, "but overall, they weren't super successful. They managed to get a baseline of powers from the Traded, and teach most how not to explode, but they didn't provide individual training, so it lacked depth. I mean, no one taught you how to push your shadows, did they?"

"No," I remembered the Margrave Academy mostly using my love of shadows to control me. "They really didn't."

"Okay, so, if you want to find out what a bunch of Traded can really do, what do you do?"

"I guess not just teach them."

"No. You *test* them. Push them. Some will die. But the strongest will live." He stopped, looked straight at me.

"I'm not that strong," I argued. "I have the right power, that's all."

"You do," Ian said. "You can manipulate shadows. That's what originally put you on the Guild of Shadows' radar." I listened with renewed interest. I'd never heard anything about why I'd been brought on board. "What if someone wanted to see how far you could push your shadows?"

"But that has nothing to do with the canister. And, besides, I'm not the only one who can manipulate them. You had some shadow snares set up here the first time I snuck in. You were a mouse," I added for good measure.

"Yes, I remember," he said. "That operative is dead."

"Oh." Pause. "Oh.

"And the old woman from the Wolf Pack League? She could do slight shadow manipulation, too."

"They took her," I whispered.

"It's a shift in pattern which worries me. She managed to push the creature back a bit, too, though not as effectively." He looked at me meaningfully. "And you're already connected to the canister. Which it seeks."

"Okay, but how would it know about me being connected to it at all?" I wracked my brain, remembering all the details I could. I wish I'd have asked Clay for more details back then. "I mean, it was Clay's contact who gave us the mission. I just tagged along. It had nothing to do with me."

"Didn't it?" he asked, his dark eyes peering at me, like he willed me to draw my own conclusions.

"Clay wanted me to join the fighter's league. He probably told them about me."

"And your powers?"

Clay would have done anything to convince them to take me. Including reveal some of my abilities.

"I don't understand any of this," I whispered.

"Neither do I," Ian said.

"Wait, you said you were worried about Sonsil?"

"Yes," he ran his hand through his hair, breaking it free from its ponytail, letting it be its usual wild self. "You should be benched," he glared at me. "You need to be benched for leaving us in the fighter's league." His voice softened. "Which, at this point, suits me just fine. Especially if this thing is in any way after you."

"I'm not in complete disagreement. I take it Sonsil disagrees?"

"He insists on keeping you active." Ian hesitated, ran his hand on the leaf of a nearby fern, as though its presence grounded him. "He's considering making you a full-fledged operative now."

My heart skipped a beat. A full-fledged operative? I could leave the Guild! Go on missions! Have more ability to control my destiny! I mean, I'd have to follow every order, but it was as free as I'd ever be! Plus, I'd get a smartphone of some sort! Have my biometrics open cool doors!

"Okay," was all I could think to say, trying not to betray my enthusiasm in the face of his worry.

"Look, don't take this the wrong way, but you're not ready, Tira, and he knows it."

"I don't see how I can *not* take that the wrong way."

"I can keep you safe if you stay under my charge," he said, ignoring me. "I can't if you're a full-fledge operative. My job right now is getting the initiates ready. I keep you safe. And I can't imagine why Sonsil would make you a full operative unless he didn't intend to keep you safe."

He paused, let go of the leaf and looked at me. "He knows you're my friend."

"He's using me against you?" I whispered. Just like they'd use Clay against me. Maybe friendships didn't pay off for the Traded.

"I'm not sure," Ian said. "I think he just wants to be able to send you into a dangerous situation without my stopping him."

"But he could *now*, couldn't he?"

Ian shrugged. "He can technically do anything he wants. But he knows I keep my people safe." Ian looked crushed at the thought of Sonsil betraying him.

"Like a mother bear?" I said with a slight smile, trying to lighten the mood.

He snorted. "If ever I'm a bear, trust me, I don't think it'll go well for any of you."

"So, what do we do?" I let the silence stretch as he pondered his options. Ian was a harsh but kind soul. I had no doubt he wanted to keep me safe. But Sonsil's will had to be followed.

"I don't know," he said softly. "I guess I just wanted you to be aware." He looked at me, as though searching for something in my eyes. I hoped he found what he looked for. "If we're both aware, we can keep each other safe."

I reached out across the empty space behind us and

held out my hand. He hesitated for half a second before taking it. His hand was rough but warm in mine.

"Let's all get out of this alive," I said. "And, in the meantime, let's go have a chat with Glitter."

He nodded, but we still held hands for a bit longer before letting go.

20

GLITTER SAT before Ian and I, hands on his knees, staring back and forth at both of us, only his eyes moving. Even his grin seemed plastered on.

"Glitter," I said, kneeling beside him. "Look, it's important you tell us what we need to know, okay?"

"Okay," he said, his eyes dropping a bit to look at me. Poor guy seemed ridiculously uncomfortable, even for him.

"How did you figure out the creature was after a piece of the portal?" Ian asked, his voice soft but steady.

Glitter glanced at me, then shifted his eyes to look at Ian. "I shouldn't say." His shoulders dropped a bit.

"Why not?" I asked.

"Because my guild doesn't want me to say."

"Glitter," I said gently. "Your guild is gone. *We* need your help now."

His ears drooped down a bit, his eyes studying his folded hands. "I liked them. My guild. They were nice."

"I'm sorry," I wished I knew how to comfort him.

"But they're gone," Ian reaffirmed. Glitter's shoulders dropped even more.

"They are," he said in his raspy voice, then seemed to gain resolve. "But I can help you?"

"Yes," Ian said. I glanced back his way. His arms were crossed, his feet firmly planted, his jaw slightly clenched, like he fought a deathly battle against impatience.

"Okay!" Glitter said, grinning again. "I overheard the guild leaders discuss it. They said that no one could find out about the monster that had been unleashed to gather the pieces of the portal. They wanted to figure out how to trap it and get the portal pieces for themselves. Good research." He nodded as he finished, as though backing their point.

He then frowned. "I guess they didn't expect the monster would find them, first."

"Thanks, Glitter." I said, looking back to Ian. I stood back up, and Glitter stared up at both of us.

"How did they know that pieces of a portal even existed," Ian asked, not sounding convinced. "Or something that might be used for a portal?"

Glitter shrugged, then held up his hands in defeat. "Research?"

Ian sighed. "Okay, well, that tells us very little, but

thank you, Glitter."

"You're welcome!" Glitter said. "Can I help more?"

"Only if you can tell us more about this monster," Ian asked, distracted as he parsed all of the information.

"No," Glitter paused. "I guess it'll be coming here?"

"Why would you say that?" Ian asked, and I groaned. Glitter had overheard Clay and I talk about the canister and had put two and two together. Hell, we might have mentioned it was a piece of the portal. I didn't remember. Glitter blended into the background too easily.

"Because you have a canister here. And the canister is for the portal?"

Ian turned toward me, eyebrow raising ever so slowly.

"I, um, well," I started.

"You talked with Clay about it and Glitter overheard."

"I was the lookout!" Glitter said.

"We don't even know what it does for sure," I mumbled.

"He's not wrong though," Ian said. "If the creature has been following a trail, then it might lead it to us."

"That's how they found the Wolf Pack League," I suddenly followed Ian's logic from earlier. How they'd been trailing *me*. "Who was the league that we stole the canister from? Was that league hit?"

Ian gave me a dark look that told me all I needed to know.

"They might not be able to trail us here," I said. "I mean, only a few people know..."

"Can you be sure no one else listened in on you and Clay?"

I flushed bright purple. "Well, no."

"We need to move," Ian said softly. "This will take some time. We must alert the Watch. And we have to figure out how to move everyone without drawing attention."

"Could we head to another guild?" I thought of Clay's League and wondered if they'd be so willing to welcome another guild, now. But I had saved them. I'd managed to stop the creature, with Glitter's help. Maybe they'd be glad to have us around.

"I'm afraid not," Ian said, dashing my blooming hopes. "The guilds are all blaming each other for the deaths, and this during our first all-guilds meeting! I don't think we'll be supporting each other again for quite some time."

"Then what? Do we wait until the creature comes for us?" I asked. *Until it comes for me?*

"We'll move as quickly as we can," Ian said. "I have to go speak with Sonsil about this. Tira..."

"I know, I know," I said. "Don't tell anyone."

"Please," then he added, for good measure. "We don't want anyone to panic."

Glitter raised his hand. Ian looked at him and nodded at him to speak.

"I'm panicking."

"Well, panic quietly," Ian said. "And keep your powers at the ready. Next time, maybe give it a suggestion to fall asleep so we can capture it?"

"Oh, that's smart," Glitter said. "No more sushi."

"Not for now," Ian turned to me. "Make sure he stays in his room. Let's keep this contained."

"Got it," I said. "But, please keep me in the loop?" He seemed poised to argue, so I added, "As a friend?"

That won him over and he nodded.

"I'll go see Sonsil now." He slipped out. The door closed behind him.

"I'll be back," I told Glitter, who folded in on himself, the fear like a weight on his back. "I promise I won't go far."

"Can Glitter come with you?"

I sighed. I wanted to head back to my room and wash up, gather my thoughts.

"I understand if not," Glitter said, lowering his head. Good manipulation. He had saved my life today. And I knew he was good at following instructions.

"Fine," I sighed. "But, try not to be too weird."

He glanced sideways, obviously confused. "Okay," he said.

I shook my head. This would have to do.

21

BARELY THREE DOORS from my room, where I could finally pull off my boots, put up my feet, and relax a bit, I heard a shout coming from Rachel's room.

No, not a shout. A scream. No, a wail.

I shared a quick glance with Glitter and we headed to her room. The door was ajar, Dame Zallir standing near it. Rachel held a piece of paper in her hand, angry tears streaming down her face, eyes deep blue with grief.

"When?" she asked, her voice shaking, the piece of paper crushed in her grip.

"Unclear," Dame Zallir said, her stern voice softened as far as I guessed it could go.

"But…this…it's… I mean, to attack them? …I need to see them," Rachel said, mourning replacing the anger.

"You can't," Dame Zallir said. "We're in lockdown,

and their bodies are being taken care of." She glanced at Glitter and I, then focused back on Rachel. "I'm sorry, Rachel. Focus on your training. Contain your anger."

She walked out without any further words.

"Rachel?" I asked, stepping into her room.

"It killed them," she said, the vitriol returning to her voice, ready to burn everything in its path.

"I'm sorry?"

"The damn monster! That thing that killed *your* guild," she pointed to Glitter, who flinched under the harsh gesture. Rachel started gathering some things and throwing them in a bag.

"Who did it kill?" Glitter asked, as though trying to strike up a conversation.

"My crew!" She wailed. "It killed all of them! It eviscerated them!" She grabbed a knife, then whipped around and threw it at the wall. "It mutilated them! Left them to rot!"

She grabbed her bag. "Out of my way! I'm going to go find it and kill it!"

"Rachel," I stood squarely in her path. She looked at me with daggers in her eyes.

"Think I can't kill it?" she asked, her skin beginning to glow as she clenched her teeth, as though swallowing the pain. "Think I won't?"

"I don't think that," I said gently, placing my hands on her arm. Warmth turned to heat. Shit. She was going to blow up unless we stopped her. Glitter looked at her with growing fascination.

"How would you even find it?" I asked, hoping to distract her.

"I don't know!" she shouted. "I'll...I don't know! I'll find a way! And I'll hold it until I explode on it, cutting it up in as many pieces as it turned my crew into!" She pulled out of my hands, her skin growing brighter, light surrounding the irises of her eyes and then filling them.

She was so distracted by her anger that she didn't notice me reaching to my belt, where my Guild insignia currently resided (barrettes weren't really my thing. Horns got in the way). I pulled free the small needle and took another step toward her.

"Tira, it killed my crew!"

"I know, and I'm sorry," I said, reaching out to her neck and pricking her gently. She never even realized what was happening, her anger dissipating into sleep, her skin regaining its natural tone.

I caught her before she struck the ground and carried her to her bed. If I'd have known a sleeping agent worked so well on her, I'd have done it in the training sessions. I sat beside her on the bed, made sure she was breathing okay. Her features were still troubled, but more peaceful.

"Will she be okay?" Glitter asked.

"Probably not, no," I answered. "But she'll figure it out."

With that, I left her on her bed to rest, and gently closed the door behind us.

Down the hallway, Dame Zallir observed our exit. Three operatives backed off as she waved them away, nodding to me before vanishing herself. They'd been ready for Rachel.

But she'd still let me head in there, to see if I could calm her down first, instead of just taking her down.

I couldn't decide if that made me feel better or worse.

22

————————

Exhausted as I was, I couldn't sleep. Glitter snored softly from the floor, but it was much more than that which kept me awake.

Rachel's crew. Clay's League. Glitter's Guild.

I felt like I'd skirted disaster every time and survived. I don't think I suffered from survivor's guilt, so much as a sense of impending doom. Any second, my luck would change and I'd lose everything.

I'd lose Clay. Ian. Hell, even Glitter.

If the creature cut me in two, it would be a gentler fate. Death would be more welcoming than living without my few friends.

I shifted again, annoyed with my inability to sleep. I sat up. Glitter didn't move, curled up half under my bed.

Well, might as well do something else to tire myself out. I stood up, quietly threw on some pants and a shirt, and exited the room. The hallways had minimal light at night, but it was easy for me to navigate in the darkness.

A soft light glowed from Rachel's room. The sleeping agent must have worn off. I debated just walking past her door, but sighed and knocked gently.

A bit of shuffling later, the door opened a crack. Rachel glared at me, but let me come in.

"Sorry about that," I whispered, sitting in her chair as she sat back on her bed, only the small table lamp casting gentle light.

"It's okay," she said. "I would have taken out half the Guild." Her pale features were drawn, her eyes shadowed by dried tears.

"Understandably," I offered. "Listen, I'm not against you leaving. I just don't want you destroying everything as you go."

She gave me a wry smile. "Thanks. That actually means a lot." Her mood darkened again, the shadows dancing around her face.

"Dame Zallir was right, though. It wouldn't help anything. They're gone, and there's nothing I can do to save them."

"I'm so sorry, Rachel." I hesitated before pushing through. "Do you have any idea why she'd have targeted your ship?

"She?"

"I saw her. Mostly."

"What did she look like?" Her words were hesitant, much more than the first time she'd asked it of me, when I'd barely seen it. I wondered if being able to imagine what slaughtered her crew would help her cope with it.

"Tall. Strong legs. Four arms like swords that can form two bigger arms with bigger swords? Her features weren't clear."

Rachel had grown still, her eyes slightly wider. "Look," I said, "she can turn invisible, and I'm pretty sure she can teleport, or something very much like teleportation. Like, she can walk through stuff and sometimes, stuff doesn't connect with her."

"In-spot teleportation," Rachel whispered. She shrugged when I looked at her questioningly. "I've heard of it."

"She's deadly," I continued, and then softened my voice. "Listen, I've seen her handiwork. It's quick, Rachel. Like, stupid quick. They probably never saw it coming. They didn't suffer, either."

Tears shimmered in her eyes, and I shifted uncomfortably.

"I'll go," I said. "But, look, if you do decide to go, just let me know, okay? So I don't worry?"

The shadows danced slightly on her face as she gave the slightest of nods. She found comfort in the shadows, too, and I liked her more for it.

I closed the door quietly behind me, leaving Rachel to her own dark thoughts.

I wandered up the hallway, everyone else apparently asleep. Near a training room, movement caught my attention. A raccoon ran across the ground, stopping near me, dark eyes staring at me intently.

"Ian?" I asked.

As an answer, he turned around and started waddling toward the training room. I followed, his tail forming a little butt target, and resisted the urge to pick him up in my arms and hug him.

I don't get nearly enough credit for all the things I *don't* do.

Raccoon Ian stopped in the training room. The walls were equipped with bands of light, currently dimly glowing green. It gave the room a magical quality, a bit like the Wolf Pack League. I smiled.

No equipment lined the room. It was specifically designed for sparring. I sat cross-legged in the middle of it, enjoying the green glow.

"Come here," I told Ian. He looked suspiciously at me, but still came over. "You are one cute raccoon," I pulled him up on my lap and patted him. He settled down. Ian retained his human thinking as an animal, but acquired some of the beast's traits, too. It made for an interesting combo.

But also a good one, because when he turned into a dog, he loved getting pats. And, apparently, so did raccoon Ian. I wove my fingers through the coarse fur, and he stretched out his sharp little claws.

"Rachel lost her crew," I whispered. "You probably already know that," I said, and he shifted his head down on my leg. "Yeah, I guessed you would."

"Clay lost a lot of friends, today. And Glitter lost his entire guild," Raccoon Ian lay very still in my lap. "We need to kill this monster, Ian," I whispered. "No matter how cool she looks."

He nuzzled my hand. I smiled and scratched his cheek. "Do you think others will get involved? Like the Watch? What about Rachel's crew? I mean, that's not a guild."

He pulled his head up and looked at me. "Were they human?" He lowered his head again, his cheek finding my fingertips. I obliged the request.

"So, won't the Watch get involved? Isn't that what you'd said? Is that good, now, or bad?" I stopped asking questions a raccoon couldn't answer. But Ian had grown very still. He looked up at me, his dark eyes impossibly wide, before lowering his head on my lap, closing his eyes slowly.

"Oh," I said, thinking I understood. "They're human, but not the right humans. Her crew didn't matter to the right people."

His little paw wrapped around my index finger.

"That's even shittier," I whispered, lowering my

head to form a shadowed veil of hair as I closed my eyes.

Nobody would grieve them except for Rachel. And, if Rachel died, nobody would grieve them at all.

Just like no one would mourn for me if my few friends were dead. The world seemed very small suddenly. And growing smaller by the second.

I focused on the breathing of the raccoon on my lap, on my own breath, and on the soft green light that made this moment seem like eternal peace, even though it felt like the world bled out and nobody knew how to bandage it.

23

I WOKE up to a gentle hand on my shoulder.

"Tira," Ian said.

I pushed the hair out of my face. Damn. Sleeping on the floor of the training room left me feeling rather stiff.

"I conked out," I said around a yawn, sitting up and stretching.

"We both did."

"I think I used you as a pillow."

"You did."

"How long ago did you shift back?" I asked. My neck hurt. Raccoons were not comfortable pillows.

"Just a few minutes ago," he said. "You rolled off of me."

"Ah. Sorry."

"It's okay," he said, sitting cross-legged beside me. "Your hair makes for a nice light blocker."

"Thank you!" I said, glad I hadn't accidentally hurt him with one of my horns. "Do you know what time it is?"

He looked down at his smartwatch. I really wanted one of those, even if it was basically a tracking device.

"Not quite evening yet, so not time to get moving," he shifted, the infinity symbol woven into his sleeve barely visible unless you knew to look for it.

"Good." I paused, hesitated. "I have a question that's been bugging me."

He waited patiently. Sometimes, I thought that Ian kept some animal traits even when he turned human. He typically didn't speak as much, or feel the need to fill in the silences. It was a good trait, but could prove a bit disconcerting.

"The old woman who got taken at the Wolf Pack League...was she one of ours?"

He shifted. "Until you're an operative, Tira, I can't tell you that kind of information."

"Right. But, like, apparently I'll be an operative soon?"

The other thing about Ian was that, much like an animal ready to attack or befriend you, the slightest movement, the slightest shift in posture, revealed a world of intention. And, right now, with the slightest tensing of his neck and lowering of the head, I knew that Ian was sad.

I placed my hand on his arm. "You've been an operative a while," I said softly. "You became one much younger than me, in fact. You're fine, and I will be, too."

He met my gaze. "I know," he spoke the words softly. "I just wish I understood Sonsil's reasoning for doing this. Why does he want to put you in danger like that?"

"Maybe he won't?"

He looked at me skeptically. "You're the only one who's managed to attack the creature. Of course he'll put you in danger. He has to, to stop the creature."

"What if I just remain an initiate?"

"Tira," Ian sounded exasperated. That made me feel better. "You can't remain an initiate. Not if you're made an operative. It's not how that works. But," he relented, "on the upside, the initiates are also moving to the main headquarters, so I'll still be there."

I smiled at him. "That'll be nice. I don't know many other raccoon pillows."

He chuckled. I liked that sound. I didn't get to hear it nearly often enough.

"How did you join the Guild, Ian?" I asked softly. "Did Sonsil recruit you?"

He shifted, bringing one knee up and resting his chin on it. "He did. Found me in a bush, years ago. Told me the Watch would find me, but he'd keep me safe."

"So you went."

"Oh no," he laughed softly again. I really loved that sound. With the green lights around us and our hushed voices, it felt like we were the only two people in the world. "I turned into a badger and bit him. Right on the hand. He still has a scar."

"Holy crap. And you lived?"

"Sonsil isn't as harsh as he seems to be..." Ian stopped, and sighed. I stared at him meaningfully. "All right. Maybe he won't get you killed. But I'm not sure. The stakes are high."

"But he's not your enemy."

"I hope not," he said.

"Why did you live in a bush?" I tried to shift the conversation away from the morose feeling that was creeping back into Ian.

I was surprised to see him hesitate.

"You don't have to talk about it if you don't want to."

"No, it's okay." He glanced at me sideways, his eyes picking up some of the green, as though he debated how to frame what he would say.

"The old woman," he said, and I frowned.

"Okay, not what I expected," I mumbled. "Was she related to you?"

"No, but she was old."

"Hence her being an old woman."

"Thank you for your contribution. Do you want to

hear this or don't you?"

"I'll be good now," I said, holding up my hands.

"She's more than twenty years old."

I remembered the Boss' words from earlier. "I had an inkling," I muttered.

"Well, not every Traded came during that one giant swap twenty years ago."

The words didn't surprise me, not after everything I'd seen. But the ramifications of it...I couldn't wrap my head around all of them. How had this happened? Why did a giant swap occur twenty years ago, then? Did humans know we existed before then?

"How come we were never told that?"

"Because the ones who all came at once...that was the first time it really became known. But there had been others, over the centuries, the millenia, even."

"Wait. Why are you telling me this?" I looked him over. He looked about my age, but he might be a bit older, I guess.

"Because I came about five years before you did, Tira. And I wasn't swapped. I was just...I don't know, transported here."

I looked at him as though seeing him for the first time. But he still looked the same to me. Same warm eyes. Disheveled hair. Thoughtful smile.

"You remember coming here?" I asked, my voice hushed with awe. I didn't. I was too little. I sometimes dreamt of another place, but it felt more like story-fueled dreams than memories. From the hellscape I saw in those dreams, I *hoped* they were just stories.

"I do," he said. "I remember landing on this world. I remember," he paused, hesitated, then pushed on, "I remember the first time I shifted into a human."

He still looked like Ian. And Ian looked human. With pale skin, brown hair, brown eyes, a little too disheveled, a little unkempt, no laugh lines surrounding his eyes…

"What were you, on your world?"

"A shifter," he shrugged. "It's weird. I don't really remember, but I remember coming over. I know the land felt differently, all soft compared to mine. And my own shapes weren't the same. I don't think fur was a thing, where I came from. Which is probably why I like shifting into furred animals. It's more comfy."

"Except hair," I teased him.

"Hair is hard! Why can't it just stay one length like everything else?"

I gave a short laugh. "Do you know others like you? Is Sonsil a Traded from another time?"

He shook his head. "As far as I can tell, Sonsil is quite human. But allied with some powerful Traded. I knew the old woman at the league. She was kind to me. Helped me master some of my shapes." He raised an eyebrow as I got a "ha-ha!" look in my eyes. So, she *had* been Guild of Shadows. "But that's it. Sometimes I spot older Traded in town, but we never talk. I don't know what to say. I don't know if it's important enough to bring up with complete strangers."

I'd spotted a few there, too, in the neighborhood dedicated to Traded. And their weapons, and shops.

"Is it lonely?" the question took both Ian and me by surprise.

He looked to the side, pondering. "Sometimes," he said. "I haven't really had friends until you," he said, "and there aren't many shared experiences with the Traded when you haven't gone to school, haven't been in a shitty family, and you remember where you come from. I never know what to talk about with other Traded, I guess. I don't know. You're not like the rest. You don't follow the rules. You have fun. You're open to the world being different than what others say it is. I guess I connected with that more than I thought I would."

He grew silent, the green light a comfortable hue around us.

"I'm glad we met," I said, meaning every word. "No matter what happens, Ian, you have a friend for life with me."

He stared at me for a good long while before he answered. "If anyone else said that, I might not believe them. But you're just stubborn enough to pull it off."

"Just don't ask me to speak in front of that many people ever again," I deadpanned.

He held up his hand, palm forward. "I promise I will

not. I can't speak for Sonsil, however. Speaking of," he said, "I should get going. We'll be starting to move people within a couple of hours. There's a lot to do."

Despite his words, he still lingered, hesitation in every limb and feature. He leaned toward me, our eyes holding contact. I held my breath.

Then the main lights turned on as the beginning of our day, aka the night, started.

He blinked, and I flushed purple. He stood up quickly, as did I.

"I'll see you soon," he gulped out and walked out of there so fast I was surprised he didn't just turn into a gazelle.

What the hell had that just been about? I'd almost kissed him. And I'd kissed Clay earlier that day. I mean, we weren't an item or anything.

But, still…

I covered my face with my hands. I knew full well that if Ian came back this moment, I'd happily kiss him, full light or not.

24

MY THOUGHTS and heart danced annoyingly as I walked back to my room, barefoot. Clay and Ian were pretty much polar opposites, but both were pretty awesome.

I hopped a couple of times to shake myself awake. It didn't matter, anyway. It's not like I'd have time for romance, now that I was about to become a full operative. I wondered what my first mission would be.

I hoped it wouldn't put Clay in danger. Or Ian.

I realized I was smiling widely.

Damn it. I was in trouble, wasn't I? Well, this wasn't entirely bad trouble to be in.

"Tira," the gravelly voice brought me back to reality and my grin faded away as I turned to see Glitter. It was nice to have one friend I didn't want to make out with.

He motioned for me to join him, right by the door to his room.

"She's here," he said, eyes wide. He pointed to the other corridor. I had no doubt who he meant.

"Stay here," I said. He shook his head, and pretty much hooked on to my arm. "Fine," I whispered as I folded the shadows around us. "But don't impede my movement."

Not that I had weapons. That would be too nice. I didn't even have boots on. Glitter seemed to sense my hesitation, and he handed me a pen. It wasn't a cheap pen, and had some weight behind it. I was pretty sure I could stab someone and do some interesting damage.

I grinned my thanks and focused on my shadows and stealth as I rounded the corner. It took everything I had not to gasp.

The warrior was in full view, not cloaked one bit. Her head almost looked like it was made from more rock, jutting out in a rectangular shape. Her body was the same flint gray as her head, but it seemed to be a shell protecting her soft, chewy center. Which was good. I could stab soft.

The rock shimmered, as though it wasn't fully there. Probably indicating that parts of her cloaking device were still active.

Her arms turned to swords just below the elbow, two on each side. All four of them were currently down. A band of metal seemed to connect each arm, maybe to facilitate the whirling attack that I'd witnessed before.

Her eyes were diamonds, hard and unwavering, as sharp as her deadly swords.

Before her, equally unwavering, stood Rachel.

I grabbed Glitter's arm, afraid he'd gasp and draw attention to us. I didn't really have to worry. He seemed to have turned to ice beside me, frozen in place at the sight.

What the hell was Rachel doing? The two stared at each other. The blue of her skin seemed muted, somehow, and all her attention was on the creature. The corridor smelled of sweets again, just like in the Galileo Guild, and like in the Wolf Pack League. Could that be another way to track her?

I hesitated. Should I attack? Should I help Rachel? But they weren't attacking each other...what the hell was going on?

Another initiate stepped out of his room, just in time to see the monster in front of Rachel. Before I could warn him, the creature held up her sword arm and swept it upwards, slicing his head in two from chin to forehead.

The creature stared at Rachel, who hadn't reacted at all to her fallen Guild member. Then, the warrior stepped away from Rachel, vanishing back into the shimmer of her cloak. And Rachel walked back in her room.

She was a traitor. She had to be! But the creature had killed her crew!

There was no time to worry about that. Why the hell hadn't the alarm sounded? There were cameras everywhere!

The creature had moved away from us, at least. I grabbed Glitter to make sure he stayed within my shadows and ran toward my room. I needed weapons. I needed shoes. And I needed to warn everyone else.

Before I could reach my room, the alarm sounded: not a distracting shrill, just a little "boomp" every two seconds. Enough to warn us, but not enough to block all our senses and overwhelm us with panic.

Initiate doors flashed once with red. It was the signal to go in and stay there. The doors would lock and keep the initiates in and, theoretically, safe.

Except when monsters could walk through walls.

It flashed again.

Rachel stepped out of her room, running down the corridor, holding a long staff in her hand, a blade fixed to its end. She hadn't seen me—I still hid in my shadows.

"Last chance," I whispered to Glitter.

"I stay with dessert," he said resolutely.

"Let's go, then."

The light flashed again, and the initiate doors all locked with a resounding clang.

I turned and trailed Rachel. If she was in league with the warrior, then she was the reason the distraction existed.

Whatever she planned, I intended to stop her.

25

RACHEL RAN DOWN THE HALL, forcing me to stay close to not lose her in the maze of corridors. Glitter didn't struggle to keep up as much as I feared he might, his back still hunched, his arms bobbing before him.

He kept up, motivated by the very real possibility that we'd get killed. I grasped my shadows tightly around me, trying to make them a bit thicker than usual to maybe even shield us from blows. For all I knew, Rachel dragged us straight into the creature's path.

What if Ian was right? What if the monster had come after me?

What if Rachel was just the lure? Using my friend against me?

My shadows faltered a bit and I pushed back my worries. Whatever I ran into, I'd figure it out when I got there. At least Glitter was with me. He could help scare the monster away, or put her to sleep.

Rachel turned a corner and slipped into the armory.

Good move.

I slowed down, grabbed the pen, and turned the corner.

Rachel was selecting a sword and a handgun. It was now or never. She could explode, sure, but I had the advantage in hand-to-hand combat. I wish I'd have refilled my sleeping agent.

I prepared to attack her and restrain her, when the perimeter of my shadows shimmered. Glitter gave a low "yip," and I grabbed my shadows and threw them with force against the creature that had encroached on them.

Apparently surprised, Rachel whipped around, firing several shots in the creature's direction. But the warrior stood ready, the bullets going through her shifted body. I moved quickly, ducking below her swords, and threw the pen in the middle of her, pushing my shadows on her.

It forced her to unshift, her stomach reforming around the pen. She looked surprised and screamed in anger, all four sword arms swinging for me. Glitter had fled, so he was of no use.

I tumbled out of the way, recalling my shadows. Rachel fired a few more shots, apparently to draw fire away from me. Thankfully, it worked.

The creature vanished.

Damn it, why had Rachel helped me? I couldn't chance her life, so I grabbed her and drew her into my shadows, pulling her down.

I motioned to her to be quiet as we hid under a table. Nothing crossed my shadows, but that didn't mean that the creature was no longer here.

I glanced at Rachel, fury and revenge flashing like lightning in her blue eyes.

Why would she ally herself with such a creature? Had she even realized what she'd done?

A thunk down the hall indicated that the creature had moved on.

"Why are you helping her?" I whispered to Rachel, holding her arm. I should have really grabbed a weapon before threatening her.

"I'm not helping her!" Rachel sounded incensed. "She killed my crew!"

"I saw you hanging out with her in front of your room," I narrowed my eyes, "and keep your voice low."

She looked puzzled and annoyed. "I...I didn't," she narrowed her eyes, looked down at her hands. "I didn't realize that...I mean, it can't be the same person, can it?"

"I know of only one sword-wielding maniac. What are you talking about?"

Rachel struggled with the weight of new knowledge. "My crew wasn't all human. We had one more Traded, Alicia. She was kind to me, Tira. Why did she kill them?"

Alicia.

"You *know* her?"

"I had no idea!" Rachel said, her voice rising again. I indicated for her to keep it down. "She's not herself! There's something wrong with her."

"No shit," I said. "Look, we have to go. Can you at least tell me that you're not allied with her? I don't think we can stop her with words."

"No," her features softened, which worried me. "I wish I could reach her, but she barely seemed to recognize me..." her eyes grew cold, her grip on her weapon tightening. "I mean, I thought maybe another Traded has some of the same abilities. She was always so gentle. I was just glad someone had survived, so I didn't want to..." she took a deep breath, her eyes closing briefly before reopening, lightning turned to steal. "We have to stop her. I can kill her."

"Great. But she'll probably kill us first."

"You can make her show herself?" she asked. I nodded and grabbed several guns, a short sword with a bit of a cross guard, and several daggers. I wish I had boots, but mostly for esthetic reasons. My feet rarely got cold.

I glanced at Rachel. She looked pale, but resolute.

"Can you do this?" I asked.

She nodded, clenching her jaw.

"Let's go," I whispered, and we stepped out of the armory. A body lay barely ten feet away, cut in two, surprise marked on the face. Rachel's face became harder, her eyes filled with growing light.

Her anger would be useful this time, if she could blow up the right person. I didn't know if it was a trick of the mind, being surrounded by metal walls and all, but I could swear the entire area smelled ever worse of iron and blood. Like the whole place had been steeped in it.

Two more bodies waited for us further down the corridor. We moved faster, while we still *had* a Guild to protect. Three more bodies, and more blood. Maybe the whole *world* was steeped in iron.

I realized where we were going, my limbs growing as cold as the dead operatives' on the floor.

She'd headed straight for the operatives' area.

Ian!

26

THE DOOR TO THE OPERATIVES' area was closed and locked, as always. Several bodies were scattered around it, and biometrics didn't exactly work for the dead. The pen I'd thrown into Alicia lay on the floor before the door.

Damn. She was definitely in there.

I pushed on the door, in case my biometrics had already been added. No luck, of course.

"How do we get in there?" I mumbled. I wondered if I could use my shadows to break it down, somehow. Maybe I could jimmy the door open with a dagger? I doubted that. There was no keyhole to pick. Just a biometric reader.

Damn tech.

Rachel reached over me, placed her hand on that section. Her skin began to glow.

"Um, Rachel?"

"Shhh," her hand shimmered and she pushed the door. A few seconds passed, the stench of blood replaced by that of melting metal. I stared at the door. Near Rachel's hand, the entire door shimmered and began to buckle.

"Push it?" she asked, still holding her hand to it. I shouldered it. The door seemed to spark against my shoulder, hyped-up static electricity crackling up and down my arm. I braced myself and pushed harder.

My skin burned where it touched the door. I should have thrown armor on, but who'd had the time? I pulled away, took a step back, then launched myself at the door with the same shoulder, pain searing as it made contact.

The door gave way, nearly sending me tumbling into two more bodies.

Rachel caught me, her still-shimmering hand burning my skin. I bit back a cry, and she quickly pulled away her hand.

"Sorry!" she whispered, looking genuinely distressed.

"It's okay," I stood back up, ignoring my burns as I folded the shadows around us. "Are you ready to do this?"

She narrowed her eyes at me and signaled that we should get going. We stepped past the two dead bodies, and I saw body parts for maybe three more on the floor.

My heart hammered in my throat. I'd just been with Ian. The green light had danced in his dark eyes, his voice soft and soothing...

Please be safe.

Rachel held her gun before her, steadying it with her right hand. It looked like a bolt gun—a mix between a shotgun and a crossbow.

Nice.

I brought up my taser gun. I hadn't gotten to use it yet, and it could be pretty damaging at full capacity. I was hoping it would knock out Alicia completely. If we could question her, find out what exactly was going on, who she worked for...not to mention what she'd done with the old woman, we might be able to stop something worse from happening.

Worse than the entire Guild of Shadows being executed where they stand.

I took another step, careful to avoid blood lazily trickling on the floor. There were no carpets to absorb the blood, here.

Glitter. I'd left him behind. He'd be fine, I told myself, trying to calm the knots in my stomach. But the creature had focused its attentions here. Probably heading toward the canister, which Sonsil undoubtedly kept in his quarters or office or something equally guarded.

Torn between stealth and speed, we moved as quickly as we could, following the trail of bodies. Alicia clearly didn't care about not being found. She knew she had the advantage, and that we were pretty much powerless to stop her.

We turned down a third corridor, and I glanced down at a movement to my left.

My heart dropped.

Ian!

A bad slash cut across his chest. His breathing was shallow, his face deathly pale. Blood gurgled up and came out in dribbles from the side of his mouth, as he tried not to choke on it.

I didn't even know if he was conscious, his eyes scrunched up in pain, his limbs perfectly still.

"Ian," I whispered at his ear. "You have to shift. You heal when you shift." I took his hand in mine. Rachel was on one knee, still within my shadows, gun at the ready as she kept an eye out.

"Ian," I pleaded, my voice choking on his name. "You have to shift. Please."

His brow furrowed, but I wasn't sure he'd heard me.

I leaned in, calling him by the first name I'd used for him, when I thought he was actually a dog.

"Max," I whispered. His fingers squeezed mine gently, and then his entire body folded onto itself, changing shape. Rachel glanced down, having never seen him shift.

"He likes privacy," I said, and she turned back to the corridor.

Soon, Max lay on the ground, a big shaggy dog that I absolutely loved. He pushed himself onto all fours, the gashes completely healed.

"Ian," I wrapped my arms around him, smelling the fur and life on him. He wagged his tail and nuzzled my neck.

Time to go. I indicated for him to stay close. He nodded. We started down the hall again. There were fewer bodies, which could be really good. Or really bad.

I stepped down another hall, uncertain where to go with the lack of trail, but Ian nuzzled me to turn left. There was no door there, just a wall. I glanced over to Rachel, who looked impatient to get going. Ian stood on his hind legs, his paw hitting a slight panel in the wall. It had looked like a decorative pattern, so I hadn't even noticed it.

Ian was right. I wasn't ready to be an operative yet.

The wall shifted sideways. And revealed pure chaos behind it.

Sonsil stood badly hurt, several Guild operatives dead at his feet. But he had managed to hold his own, sparks flying as his twin swords met the creature's invisible blades.

I gathered my shadows and slammed them toward him, revealing Alicia in all her glory. Sonsil took the advantage, kneeling and striking her legs before rolling away, leaving a trail of his own blood.

Ian growled and jumped after Alicia, going for her neck, but there was no soft flesh to get hold of—it was all rock-hard. He leapt away, landing on his feet before propelling himself further as swords came crashing down.

I tightened my shadows around her. Maybe I could hold her there, if I tried hard enough...she turned on me, her eyes narrowing. She knew I was the one doing this.

Where the hell was Glitter and his damn suggestions? Probably under my damn bed.

"Alicia," Rachel called out, grief in her voice. "Whatever's making you do this, you're stronger than it. Fight back!"

For a second, Alicia focused on Rachel, and something else seemed to shine in those diamond eyes.

They didn't seem so cold.

"Alicia, please!" Rachel pleaded. "I don't want to lose you, too!"

Alicia's arms shifted sideways, losing their attack position. But she didn't answer, as though trapped in a miasma of indecision. The entire room became flooded with the scent of sugar and sweets, a sickly layer over the stench of death.

Sonsil took advantage of her confusion, striking her

in the back. Rachel screamed. Alicia screamed. I think I screamed.

The blades came back up, shredding parts of Sonsil's coat as he fell back, Ian growling in front of him, standing guard.

I ran to them, throwing my shadows up around Alicia, trying to stop her from moving. To hold her steady.

To stop her from killing anyone else.

She planted her right leg down and pushed, all four arms coming up like shields against herself as she tried to cloak again. She pushed to break my shadows.

I screamed, pulling the shadows from all around, as far as I could go. From the floors above and below, from the bodies still bleeding out, from the minute cracks in the seemingly perfect metal surfaces...but Alicia pushed through.

Ian growled beside me, his fur on end, but he couldn't stop her.

Sonsil struggled to stand back up, with little success.

"You killed my crew," Rachel spat out from the other side of her. "*Our* crew!" She took a step toward her, throwing aside her gun as her skin began to glow.

"Rachel!" I said, ducking as Alicia came close. I managed to push her back with my shadows, her limbs straining against their strength. I surrounded her with shadows, every crack revealed and brought to light.

On the metal band surrounding her chest, I thought I spotted, etched in it, a guild symbol. My blood ran cold.

"Rachel, wait..." before I could stop her, Rachel screamed, pink shimmers gliding on the air around her.

"I won't let you kill another crew!" She screeched in anger and grief, light exploding from the shimmers.

"Down!" I screamed, and threw myself to the ground, keeping my shadows around Alicia, hoping she wouldn't have the chance to strike before Rachel exploded.

Rachel unleashed all of her powers at once, a great shockwave pummeling into us. I lost track of Ian and Sonsil, and Rachel, and even myself as I went flying right out of the room.

I'm pretty sure I lost consciousness, or nearly, and only recovered my senses when a dog licked my face. Ian whined as I opened my eyes and pushed myself up on my elbow.

"I'm okay," I said, patting him. He sat down beside me, looking back into the room. I could see straight outside where a massive hole had been punched into the side of the building. I could also see three floors up, and three below. Rachel had managed to pull herself back toward the wall, but hadn't exited the room, a bit of floor still holding her up.

Sonsil stood, looking fierce and proud despite being

covered in blood. He sheathed both swords on his back, then helped Rachel up and out of the precarious room.

"I think," Sonsil said, "that that did it."

As if to punctuate his words, one of the sword arms tumbled down from where it had landed, three floors up.

It was definitely over.

Which was great, because every part of me hurt.

Rachel closed her eyes, as though saying a silent prayer, or imagining she was on the sea, far away, with her crew alive, happy, and laughing by her side.

ALL THINGS CONSIDERED, we'd been lucky. The injured filled the infirmary, meaning lots of people had survived. We'd lost an entire chunk of the building, but we were just leaving anyway.

Not too bad, for a day's work.

Per his request, I stayed near Sonsil, as Ian seemed trapped in dog form for now. Following the attack and the destruction of most of the operatives' section of the Guild, they were getting ready to move. Humans would come soon, to see what the hell had happened to the building. The fewer Traded here, the better.

Rachel had left for the infirmary, having burned herself with her own explosiveness. My burns weren't bad, and none of my injuries stung too hard.

Ian sat beside me, and I petted him as I looked around, testing the shadows. Parts of Alicia were still cloaked, but I could highlight them for others to see. The trick was in scouring the entire floor.

"Another foot," I said, pleased I'd found it. She'd exploded everywhere, so it wasn't easy work. Our main worry was that someone would trip on a cloaked sword arm and lose a foot.

I pushed my shadows up. "There!" A piece of arm embedded in the wall by the force of the explosion.

Operatives followed my trail and packed the pieces in special containers. We had three out of four arms, but the last one proved elusive.

"Do you want me to go down?" I asked Sonsil, looking at the shattered room.

"No," he said. "The building isn't that stable anymore, so we should make our exit," he turned from me to the operatives, indicating that the body parts containers should be placed in the third door to the right, where "special" transport would be arranged.

I imagined the canister was there, too.

"Everything safe?" I asked Sonsil, raising an eyebrow.

He looked at me as though to say he didn't need to answer me, but relented. "Yes. We'll start by moving the initiates. Then the operatives and special transport."

"Perfect," I said. "And the wounded?"

"With the initiates," Sonsil said. "Are you concerned about your friend?"

I looked down to Ian, then realized he meant

Rachel. Could I trust Sonsil? I placed my hand on Ian's head. Sonsil had found Ian and kept him safe. He'd protected him from the world, given him a place to stay, a purpose.

But even Ian wasn't sure if he could trust Sonsil.

I held my peace, choosing not to tell him that I'd seen Rachel talking with Alicia. After all, hadn't Rachel just killed her? I just didn't know if Sonsil would use the information for other means.

There had been enough betrayals today, and this information hardly seemed important.

Not anymore.

"I'll go check on her," I said, and then added. "If you don't need me here anymore?"

"No," he said. "Ian can oversee the transport here. I believe I'll head to the infirmary myself," he said. He was covered in his own blood, his shirt slashed in several placed.

"That's probably a good idea," I said.

"A good operative is a living one, after all," he said with a wince. He gently patted Ian and then shuffled his way toward the infirmary. I watched him go. He'd put up a good fight. He might be human, but he was a highly trained human.

"I'll be back," I knelt beside Ian, looking deep into his eyes. I could see him, there. I could see his intelligence and gentleness. He'd almost died on me. If he hadn't shifted…

I forced the thought away and hugged him. "Be careful," I said. "I'll see you soon."

He licked my cheek and I laughed as I stood up and, without a second glance back, headed to my room.

It was time to pull Glitter out from wherever he'd hidden himself.

THE LIGHTS WEREN'T on in my room when I opened the door, which worried me. Glitter couldn't see in the dark. At first glance, I couldn't see him beside my bed. I knelt beside it.

"Glitter? Are you in here?" *Please be in here.* What if he'd been caught by Alicia and I'd been too busy running around to notice?

"Glitter?" I peered under the bed.

I saw him there. Two green eyes shining, looking back at me.

"It's okay, Glitter," I said gently, holding out my hand to help him out. "The monster is gone."

The two eyes focused on me, unblinking. They seemed steady. Too steady. Something was different about them, but before I could place it, Glitter spoke. His voice wasn't raspy anymore.

"Are you sure about that, Tira?"

I DREW my shadows around us, though I wasn't sure why. I really needed to get to the special shipment, without being seen. Glitter walked behind me, silent as we went by operatives and initiates, the place bustling with the noises of imminent departure.

The whole place breathed more easily. We'd been under the threat of attack for days now and, now that it was gone, everyone seemed more relaxed. Grieving, yes. In shock, certainly. But also more relaxed.

Like we'd gotten to the end of a book, and finally knew who would die and who would live, so we could enjoy the last denouement in peace.

This is a strange line of thought.

Wrapping the shadows more tightly, I kept walking, as though in a dream. Maybe this *was* a dream, and there would be cake at the end.

Cake with icing and sugar and those fun flowers...

No. That wasn't right. This wasn't a dream.

I'd smelled sugar before, in the Galileo Guild, before the creature hurt me.

Before the creature cut me, but didn't kill me.

I tried to focus my mind, to think about where I was going and why, but those threads evaded me. I just needed to get to the operatives' section. To the special shipment, before it left.

I saw the creature. I could tell the guild members about it. They came together to form a plan.

Because of cake.

Because of cake.

The door leading to it was closed. I placed my hand on the biometrics pad, and it opened.

It seemed my promotion had come through, probably to help with the movement of everything now that so many operatives were dead.

I'd get more freedom. More equipment! Missions!

I'll get to visit Clay.

Why was I so sad? Where was I? I'd walked up the corridor. I needed to remember something important.

The sugar is in your mind and in his mind and you're not you break free break free

Wait. Was that Ian, sitting before the closed door, keeping a sharp eye out, waiting patiently for the transport to come? To take the body parts away...and whatever treasures the Guild of Shadows hid here. And the canister.

The canister!

Oh no. *No no no.* I tried to break free, but a hand reached the back of my head, and I couldn't stop the shadows from forming more thickly around us, hiding us.

I managed to moan just a little bit.

Ian looked up, cocked his head sideways. I couldn't make more noise, and I stopped walking, held in place by a power I couldn't see.

But Ian stood now. He could smell me. His tail wagged once, then stopped. A growl erupted from his jaw.

Glitter's hand flicked, a dart hitting Ian in the chest. He slumped to the ground, soundless.

Ian. I couldn't scream his name. We started walking again, and I couldn't even turn to look at him, to make sure he was all right.

"You made this too easy," Glitter said as I opened the door to the special shipment. Damn biometrics!

"I've been following you since the first guild where you found me. I knew you'd lead me to the canister, eventually. I figured one purple demon was enough for a world to hold, and you were the one who stole the canister, along with your buddy Clay. A slight suggestion to make sure you survived the first battle, and you led me straight where I needed to go, if a bit of a circuitous route." He looked at me. "Wait here," he ordered, and I did, standing by the door.

I tried to move my arm, but couldn't. Somewhere behind me, Ian lay on the ground. Breathing proved difficult, my breaths unable to accelerate to match my mounting distress, my heart pumping increasingly quick and my lungs struggling to meet the demand.

I felt lightheaded and swallowed hard, trying to calm myself so I didn't pass out.

"But Ian, well, he was a gift," Glitter said as he pulled the canister out. He tossed it into his shoulder bag and stood before me. Gone were his bent back and his broken gait. Gone were his glowing green eyes, and his hesitant movements. I managed to move my hand, just a bit.

I really wanted to strangle him.

"Nice," he said, seeing my hand twitch. He looked thoughtful. "I'm sorry we won't get to hang out anymore, for what it's worth."

I wished I could spit in his face. He held out his hand, and his bandages slithered off him, revealing covered arms underneath, in some kind of dark green fabric.

The bandages wrapped around my arms and legs, binding them tightly. Glitter pushed me over, but softened my fall with his leg.

"Why?" I managed to say in between breaths, his

control beginning to fade. The world no longer smelled like dessert.

Dessert. That's what he'd called me. I thought he was scared. That he needed me. Needed a friend. I tried to care for him. To look out for him.

I hated him.

"We all have our role to play," he said, his voice now strong and in full control.

"I saved you!" my voice sounded as raw as my emotions.

"No," he said. "I was never a part of the Galileo Guild." He bent down, so he would be closer to me. I struggled to stand up, but the bonds held me tight. "I just needed to get your Guild to come play."

His eyes narrowed. His dark, non-glowing eyes. These eyes were filled with purpose. Cold, calculating purpose.

I missed Glitter. I missed the glowing green eyes. I missed my weird little friend.

"Do you ever wonder if it's all necessary?" he whispered, as though speaking to himself. "Do you wonder if we really need the guilds?"

"It's how we live in peace with humans," I said.

"Is it?" He asked, raising an eyebrow. The bandages around his face were also slipping away. I could see skin beneath them, though I couldn't make out a color. All that I knew for sure was that he was Traded. "How come the ones who came before us got to just slip in as part of the population?"

"What?" I asked, trying to buy time as I worked on the bonds behind my back. I dislocated a thumb when he looked away for a split second, hoping he didn't see the pain flash across my face. That was one trick that didn't get easier.

"There's a reason these guilds were formed, and I doubt keeping us in line is even the main one."

Even with the thumb completely out, I couldn't work my hands free. The bandages wrapped too tightly up my arms, too. Tears of frustration sprang to my eyes.

"What do you want with me?"

"With you?" He asked, surprised. "Well, this," he showed me the container.

"But… you took the old woman who could also fold shadows."

"Yes," he said, nodding. "But that's a feature, not the main selling point. The fact that she didn't come twenty years ago, well, now *that* I'm interested in."

I moaned slowly. He didn't want me. I'd just been the path to the canister. He wanted Ian. *A gift.* I struggled more fiercely against my bonds, but everything hurt, and they didn't even shift under my efforts.

"Listen," the man who I could no longer call Glitter said as he stood up, perfectly straight. "I don't mean you harm, but others do. They will come. The Guild of Shadows has accumulated too many secrets already. They will not be able to contain them."

He hid the canister back in his hoody. "No more than this canister can contain what's needed next."

"Why do you need it?" I asked, feeling him slip away from me. I needed answers. I needed to know what he intended to do with it. With Ian, still unconscious beside me, tongue lolling out of his doggie mouth.

"For the next steps, Tira," he picked up Ian, cradling the dog in his hands.

"Let him go!" I screamed, thrashing against the bonds, pulling my hand through, but too slowly. The bonds seemed to be releasing, just like his control over my mind had evaporated.

"Don't follow us," the man said, and he vanished.

I pulled my hand free. "Ian!" I screamed, but the corridor stood empty, and not even my echo bothered answering me.

29

I SAT in my room in the new-to-me Guild of Shadows. The transport here had been a blur. I hurt. They'd patched me up, but the bandages had cut deep, and the burns had begun to peel.

My heart hurt most of all. I didn't know what to do with the grief. Ian had been right there. *Right. There.* And I couldn't save him.

I told him we'd be friends forever. But forever counted on both of us being alive.

What are they doing to you, Ian?

A knock came at my door. I swallowed hard, and before I could fully compose myself and open it, Sonsil stepped in.

I started to stand, but he indicated to me to remain seated. He took the chair opposite me, his elbows on his knees. He looked tired.

Old, even. Like the battle and loss of so many operatives had sapped him of strength.

"We can't find any trace of Ian," he said softly. "We looked everywhere. I've had every remaining operative seek him out, but no luck."

He sounded genuinely grief-stricken. Why had Ian not trusted him?

"I should have been able to keep him safe," I muttered, not looking at him. I couldn't bear to see the weight of loss crush his proud shoulders.

"Ian would have done anything to protect you," he said. "I've never known him to have a friend. It distracted him."

"That's why you wanted to separate us," I practically spat out. "Get me killed in action so he'd be back to his full potential again?"

He gave a low chuckle, taking me by surprise. "Of course not," he said. "I'd have posted you to the backwoods somewhere, if it would have helped keep him safe. Less distracted."

"If we stopped separating each other, if we stopped breaking allegiances instead of tightening them, we'd be stronger for it," I rebutted, remembering the guilds just falling apart after one attack.

"Like with Glitter?"

"No. He was a traitor. But not everyone is like that. I refuse to believe that. Just like Rachel isn't. Nor is Clay. Besides," I softened my voice, "you cared for Ian.

It didn't weaken you. It made you stronger. Made you try harder to protect him."

He looked at the ground, seconds trickling by in silence, the grief that washed off of him smothering the air out of the room.

"It doesn't matter, now," he eventually said. His back straightened, his face no longer betraying his emotions. He had assumed his role as leader again. "What's done is done."

"We have to get him back," I said softly, not yet having shuttered my grief away. I didn't know how. And I didn't want to learn.

"No," he said, but his voice softened. "I can't. I have to worry about the Guild of Shadows. We need to figure out what exactly is at the heart of this conspiracy. And who killed so many Traded. We must focus to maintain the balance."

"Ian is at its heart, Sonsil," I gritted my teeth. "We have to save him!"

"No, he's just a small part of it," regret coated every word. He took a deep breath, refocused on me. "I cannot follow him." He looked at me pointedly. "Nor should we be aware of anyone else doing so. If anyone would try, we would have to declare them rogue. That would surely mean their death at the hands of the Watch."

"What's the Watch?" I stood alert now. The air, crushed by grief just moments ago, now felt electrified.

"Some of the oldest Traded, come over centuries ago, formed the Watch. To keep everyone in line. They established the guilds to keep the new Traded in check. They will not hesitate to kill to maintain a semblance of order."

That sounded dangerous. "I understand," I said. All the anxiety I'd felt over losing Ian vanished into this simple statement. Sonsil couldn't go after Ian. But I could.

And I would go after Ian, no matter what.

Sonsil stood, as did I. He placed a hand on my shoulder and locked eyes with mine, squeezing my shoulder.

"Be safe," he said so softly I strained to hear.

"You, too," I whispered back, for good measure.

His hand was gone, the vulnerability vanished from his eyes, and he became all business again. He walked out of my room without another word or glance back.

I wondered if I'd ever get to know him better. Or see Ian again.

I would. I had to. I had to find Ian and bring him home.

This world felt too empty without him in it.

EPILOGUE

I ENTERED THE MISSION ROOM, unchallenged by anyone, simply receiving a few nods. My tail swished slightly behind me, but I didn't pay it any mind. My focus lay elsewhere, as I sat at a briefing station.

I'd been right. The operatives' mission rooms were much cooler. Black walls cocooned us in, screens all around for surveillance. Several guilds were on the monitor now, including a fight Clay was currently owning. I grinned at it, seeing his joy.

He'd hate knowing how much of an eye we kept on his league. On his friends.

On all of the Traded.

I placed my hand on my desk's scanner. A screen flickered to life. I tapped on the area maps, monitoring any strange activity reported by humans. It was normal operative behavior, or so my two days as one had taught me.

But I was looking for specific errant Traded behavior. Someone doing things like in a dream, even though they might not want to. Trying to track down Not-Glitter, which would lead me to Ian.

I'd looked deep into the records, too, and for the past twenty years you could track him, here and there. All over the world. He'd been here a while. And up to something since the portals had opened up.

Rachel's crew had been targeted because they'd carried the container to the initial guild. I don't think she'd even known. I'd tell her, eventually. Probably.

If it became necessary.

Right now, all that mattered was tracking Not-Glitter. And the canister.

And Ian.

All trails would lead to him.

If one good thing came out of me becoming an operative, it was the power to access the full information network of the Guild of Shadows.

And then, I'd find Glitter.

And give him hell.

-The End-

The adventures of Tira Misu will continue in
The Guild of Shadows 3: Hell Bound*!*

ABOUT THE AUTHOR

Marie Bilodeau is an Ottawa-based author and storyteller, with eight published books to her name. Her speculative fiction has won several awards and has been translated into French (Les Éditions Alire) and Chinese (SF World). Her short stories have also appeared in various anthologies. In a past life not-so-long ago, she was Deputy Publisher for The Ed Greenwood Group (TEGG). Marie is also a storyteller and has told stories across Canada in theatres, tea shops, at festivals and under disco balls. She's won story slams with personal stories, has participated in epic tellings at the National Arts Centre, and has adapted classical material.

Marie is co-host of the Archivos Podcast Network with Dave Robison, co-chair of Ottawa's speculative fiction literary convention CAN-CON with Derek Künsken, and is a casual blogger at Black Gate Magazine.

Find out more and see pretty book covers at www.mariebilodeau.com.